The Singing Place

Coleman Luck

The Sandstar Group

The Sandstar Group
POB 3613
Oakhurst, CA 93644
www.colemanluck.com

Publisher's Note: This is a work of fiction. Names, characters, places, and incidents are a
product of the author's imagination. Locales and public names are sometimes used for
atmospheric purposes. Any resemblance to actual people, living or dead, or to business-
es, companies, events, institutions, or locales is completely coincidental.

Book Layout ©2013 BookDesignTemplates.com

Editing by Coleman Luck, lll
Cover Design by Carel Gage Luck

ISBN:9780988888876

Dedicated to the memory of my little sister,
Virginia May Luck,
whose life was so limited,
but whose influence was so profound.

Contents:

Introduction

The essence of this story has haunted me for almost 40 years. Over the years, it has taken different forms. Since I am a screenwriter, at the beginning I wanted to tell it in a theatrical film. The first version, written about 1979 or 80, was one of the early professional screenplays of my Hollywood career.

Along the way, various friends have believed in the story and tried to assist in seeing it produced for the screen. The first was my old friend and Academy Award winning composer, Al Kasha. There have been others. Twenty years ago, ABC even contracted with me to adapt a version of it into a script for a one hour dramatic television pilot. Sadly, it didn't go beyond script stage. A dozen years ago, I decided to put it into a "final" scripted form. My wife, Carel, and I co-wrote it as a two-hour film. It is from that version that the story you are about to read was taken.

To all who have walked with me at various stages of the long journey called The Singing Place, please accept my gratitude.

What you are about to read is a simple story, simply told, that has been close to my heart for a long time. When you read the memorial at the end, you will understand why. But on a larger level, The Singing Place represents a longing for all things to be made right in the world, for every hurt to be healed.

As a follower of Jesus Christ, the King, I look forward to the wonderful day when that will happen.

Coleman Luck
In the Sierra Nevada Mountains near Yosemite
Summer 2013

CHAPTER ONE

Goodbye

A rocker creaked slowly back and forth on a hard-wood floor. And as it creaked, there was humming. A rasping, trembling voice hummed a rigid pattern.

Four notes, over and over.

Four notes without variation.

Four notes starting low, then rising and falling, on and on as though they would never end.

In broken time with the humming, a pair of scuffed men's shoes pushed the rocker upward. The sole on one was built up an inch higher than the sole on the other. As the shoes pushed, the rocker rose and the shoes rose with it.

Pushing...

Rocking...

Humming...

In a small, shadowed bedroom a forlorn figure sat rocking and humming. His shoulders were hunched and his head hung down. Though not a child, he clutched a large children's book and a worn blanket folded to perfection. These were gripped tightly as though they might fly away. Alone, he sat in a room that was empty except for the rocking chair.

And the chair creaked.

And the shoes scraped.

And the voice kept humming.

Eddie Gartman was 26 years old, but his mop of blonde hair was uncombed like a little boy and his t-shirt and pants looked like he had slept in them. As he hummed, his eyes glanced back and forth in a rigid pattern that followed the notes. Right, then left, then right again.

Childhood that wasn't childhood lay gently on Eddie's face. Being short, at first glance, many people mistook him for a child...until they saw his eyes. For anyone who cared to look into his eyes, the truth was visible. Around them were lines of age and sorrow. But most people never saw his eyes, because he kept his head hanging down. Even when he raised it, his true age was masked by the severe softness of the Touch of God that the medical profession calls Down Syndrome.

Little boy.

Young man.

Old man.

In this world, but not of it.

Lifting one hand from the blanket and book, Eddie rubbed his forehead and kept rubbing. He always did that when he was nervous. And this day, he was more than nervous. He was afraid. This day, the whole world was clanging and crashing. So he rocked and hummed and rubbed to make it all go away.

The door to the bedroom opened and a harried woman entered. Julie Gartman, Eddie's sister, was 38 years old, and attractive, but life had been hard. In her eyes was the shadow of the worst kind of sorrow, the sorrow of regret. This day of all days, that sorrow was close to the surface.

"Okay, honey, you ready to go?"

From Eddie, there was no response, not even a look. His shoulders remained hunched and his head didn't move.

Rocking and humming and rubbing.

"Eddie, it's time to go. We have to leave."

Four notes over and over, with eyes glancing right, then left, then right again.

"Sweetie, you can't stay here any longer. Look around. Everything's gone. We've moved it all out."

The only answer she got was that he stopped rubbing and gripped the blanket and book tight, as though they too might be taken.

"Eddie, don't do this to me. I know you can hear me. Now we're going for a ride in the car. On the way, we'll stop and get ice cream. How about that? Does that sound good?"

Nothing. It was as though she didn't exist.

"EDDIE, talk to me." Julie fought back tears and her voice broke. "Please, Eddie, I need you to help me today."

The rocking and humming stopped. The head lifted, but the eyes stared at nothing.

"Can't. Can't-can't."

His sister knelt beside him. "Why not, honey? Why can't you?"

"Mr. Bunley."

"But Mr. Bunley's right here. He's going with us."

She showed him the front of his book. On the cover was the picture of a funny little gnome-like man dressed in colorful rags and wearing a floppy hat. Beneath his dancing feet was the title, "Mr. Bunley's Happy Singing Place."

With great conviction, Eddie shook his head back and forth, "Mr. Bunley says, no."

Bending close, Julie laid her head next to his. "Sweetie, I know how you feel. I love this house too. But I can't leave you here. There's no one to take care of you. Don't you understand? Mom isn't here anymore and I can't afford to keep the place."

Eddie's head shook back and forth very fast. *"Mr. Bunley says, no! No, no, no! Can't go! Can't! Can't! Can't!"*

"Oh, God..." Julie rose and looked down at him. "Eddie, if you don't get out of that chair and come with me right now, I'm going to get Alex and Steve and they're going to carry you out. I don't want to do that, but I will. Do you understand me?"

He just kept shaking his head.

"They're right outside waiting."

The humming started again, this time much louder and with a very stubborn new persistence, which included sticking out his jaw, pursing his lips and closing his eyes.

"All right, if that's the way you want it." She left the room.

The moment Eddie was alone, he huffed out his breath, ballooning his cheeks and started rubbing his forehead again.

The door opened and Julie returned, this time with two very large, very self-conscious, African-American teenagers.

"Here they are, Eddie. Now are you coming or are they going to carry you out? There are lots of people outside and it's going to look pretty funny if we have to carry you like a baby. If you don't want that to happen, you've got to get up right now."

There was no response, so she nodded to the teenagers. As they moved reluctantly toward the chair, Eddie stopped rocking and very, very, very slowly began to stand up.

"Okay. Okay-okay-okay-okay-okay. *Okay!*"

Breathing sighs of relief, the boys withdrew from the room. As soon as they were gone, Eddie paused, bent over, with his butt still above the chair.

"No, you don't. Don't you sit back down. They haven't left. They're right outside."

With his butt still suspended, Eddie began thoroughly brushing off his clothes for no apparent reason.

"And don't you start that either. I know this game. It can go on for 45 minutes. Come on!"

As he continued brushing, Julie took his arm and led him authoritatively toward the door. He walked with a slight limp.

"My chair, my chair."

"We're going to bring your chair later today. You will have it with you. I promise."

Together they passed through the living room of a modest Los Angeles home. Like the bedroom, it was empty. As they headed toward the front door, Eddie continued brushing himself. Just as they were about to go outside, he stopped brushing and took one last look at his home. As Julie watched, it was all she could do to hold back the tears. After a long look, he turned away.

Eddie and Julie stepped out onto the front porch. On the lawn, a yard sale was in progress. Strangers were pawing over the remains of a lifetime. Rose, the mother of the teenage boys, was managing the sale for Julie.

Eddie was startled by all of it. As though in a daze, he let Julie lead him down the steps. Slowly, they passed between lamps and couches, around chairs and tables, then through rows of boxes filled with memories. The shoppers stared at him. A little girl pointed. Her mother pulled her away.

Eddie and Julie walked on, past everything that Eddie had known all of his life. His eyes lingered, but he didn't say a word.

Finally, they came to a table covered with old Christmas ornaments, ANY FOUR $1. Nearby, stood an artificial tree with faded flocking. A tag on a branch read $6 or best offer.

Eddie paused and stared at the remains of Christmas. Then, slowly, he picked up a single tiny ornament from the table. It was a miniature manger scene. Holding it close to his eyes, he scrutinized it, but then his hand began trembling. With the utmost care, he put the ornament in his shirt pocket and turned away.

Tears were streaming down Julie's face. As Rose walked up to them, there were tears in her eyes, too.

"Goodbye, Eddie. We love you. We'll come see you on Christmas. I'll bring you some gingerbread cookies."

She hugged him, but there was no response. His eyes were vacant as though he didn't know she was there.

Julie led him past a real estate "For Sale" sign, to a ten-year-old Chevy mini-van parked in the drive.

Wiping the tears away, she turned to Rose, "I'll be back in a couple of hours."

"You take your time, honey. We'll be right here. Everything's fine. We're praying for both of you."

"Thanks."

Eddie climbed into the front passenger seat and stared out the window at the people and the furniture. Julie got in and started the engine, then backed carefully into the street.

In the yard, the shoppers continued their pawing. An old man pulled out his money and picked up the Christmas tree.

As they drove away, Eddie's face was framed in the window. As long as he could, he kept watching, until the house that he had known forever vanished into the past.

CHAPTER TWO

Mr. Bunley

Rush hour on the Hollywood Freeway and the steel herd was jammed solid. Julie's mini-van crept along a foot at a time. "Joy to the World" started playing over the radio. A car in the next lane cut her off.

Blasting her horn, she yelled, "JERK!"

Unable to stand the music, she turned it off. "Dear God, I hate Christmas."

Taking a deep breath, she struggled for control, then started talking, mostly to herself.

"Eddie, you're gonna love this place. I just know you will. The people are so nice. You'll have lots of friends. And they go on trips--like to the zoo, and movies and Disneyland. Once you're there for a while, you won't want to leave. That's what all the parents say."

He wasn't looking at her, so he didn't see the tears that came again.

"Oh, Eddie, it's so hard. I can't take care of you. I can barely take care of myself, I'm such a mess. I don't even know where my next month's rent is coming from. I could be out on the street in a few weeks. Helping mom at the end, I couldn't keep my job. I've got to find a new one right away. But you're gonna be all right, sweetie. You don't know what this means, but the money from the house is yours. Mom and I set it up so that, no matter what happens, you'll always be taken care of."

She wiped her eyes, "Mom picked out a room for you. You're going to come to my apartment and visit every other weekend. As long as I've got an apartment. And we'll be together for Christmas and your birthday, I promise. And I'm going to make sweet potato pie just like mommy did..." But the tears wouldn't let her go on.

Suddenly, Eddie's attention jerked up to the sunroof. Onto his face came a broad grin. He jabbed a stubby finger upward.

"Hey-hey-hey-hey. Mr. Bunley, Mr. Bunley. Up-up-up-up-there. Up there."

Julie shook her head, "Oh God, here we go."

"Open it, open it, can-I, can-I?

This was a game that had been played a hundred times. She was too weary to argue, "Oh, all right."

Eddie pushed the button and the sun roof slid open. Instantly, all of his attention focused on an imaginary friend who seemed to have dropped into the seat next to him.

"Ha, ha, ha, ha. Look. Look. Mr. Bunley."

Julie mumbled, "Yes, hello to Mr. Bunley."

"Uh oh, uh, oh. Jumping, jumping." Eddie twisted around to stare at the back seat.

"Mr. Bunley, in-the-back. In-the-back. Can-I? Can-I?"

"Eddie…"

"Please…please-please…"

"If you start jumping back and forth you're going to get me a ticket."

"But Mr. Bunley, Mr. Bunley…"

She glanced in her mirrors. No cops around. "God help me, if I could see Mr. Bunley I'd strangle that little freak. Whoever wrote that book, I want to kill him. Oh, all right, but you can't crawl back and forth. When you're there, you sit down and buckle up, do you hear me?"

Croaking with laughter, Eddie lumbered over the seat. In the process, he stuck a leg in front of Julie's face.

"Eddie...I'm gonna have an accident."

He had barely fallen into the back, when he started yelling and laughing and crawled to the front again.

"Stop it, Eddie. Stop this right now. I said, no crawling back and forth."

"Mr. Bunley tickling. Stop-it, stop-stop-it, stop-it, Mr. Bunley."

While Eddie laughed, Julie started to sob. Then, he stopped crawling. Crouching on the floor in the rear, he whispered to his invisible friend, "I-know-I-know-I-know-I-know-I-know-I-know...Now? Right now? Right-right-right-right-now? Scared."

"Eddie, get off the floor and buckle your seatbelt."

But he didn't. Instead, he kept whispering, "Scared-scared. Okay-okay-I-do-it. I-do-it."

Incredibly excited, he grabbed his book and stared at it. "Gotta-find it, gotta-find-it-gotta-find-it. Right-right-right-now..."

"Eddie, did you hear me? Don't make me stop this car..."

But the car was already stopped in the traffic. Clutching the book and blanket, suddenly, Eddie lunged for the door and threw it open.

Julie screamed, *"Eddie, what are you doing?"*

As she twisted around trying to grab him, her foot slipped from the brake to the gas pedal. The station wagon lurched forward crashing into the car in front of her. Leaping out, Eddie ran through the traffic, then up the freeway embankment.

The man Julie hit got out of his car. Jumping from hers, Julie ran after Eddie.

"Eddie, come back..."

The other driver yelled, *"Hey, where are you going?"*

But Julie didn't stop. With horns blaring, she ran between the cars. Eddie was moving with surprising speed. When she reached the embankment, he vanished into the heavy bushes at the top. Struggling up the slope, finally she pushed through.

"Eddie..."

But the street in front of her was empty. Her brother was gone.

CHAPTER THREE

Jorge

In the semi-darkness of a shabby studio apartment, a man lay sleeping on a cot. Suddenly, a clock radio went off with ranchero music playing a very loud rendition of "Feliz Navidad." The man groaned. Reaching over, he pounded the thing to silence, then sat up, bleary-eyed.

Jorge Mendoza looked a decade older than his 40 years. There was gray in his black hair and his hands were gnarled. Beneath the ravages of a hard life there was kindness in his eyes that whispered of something very deep and strong.

Trying to wake up, Jorge rubbed his face and stared around. His apartment had no furniture except the cot, a metal chair and a work table. But there was much more. Hanging from the walls and ceiling was a wonderful collection of patchwork puppets, each one a little masterpiece, created with a distinctly Colombian flare. There were furry monsters, monkeys and dragons, children with big mouths and smiling eyes, a horse, a pig and a dog and many more, all hand-made from a pile of scraps and odd pieces stacked in the corner. Several puppets lay on the work table in early stages of creation.

Next to a half-finished clown, sat the photograph of a dark, attractive woman holding a little girl. Near the picture stood a tiny Christmas tree.

Still barely awake, Jorge stumbled through the puppet menagerie to the bathroom. Staring at himself in the mirror, he fumbled for a can of shaving cream. After smearing it on his face, he rinsed his hands, then lifted a razor.

He was about to make a stroke, when another face appeared beside his in the mirror. It was fat and furry with a bulbous nose, large eyes and thick glasses. The face stared intently at him.

He turned toward it, "Yes? You want something?"

The puppet tilted its head and spoke in a deep raspy voice, "You are very ugly. Shaving will not help."

"And I suppose you think you are beautiful?"

"Yes, very beautiful."

"I'm glad you like yourself so much. If you don't mind, I'd like a little privacy. I have to get ready for work."

"No work today. We're going fishing."

"We're not going fishing."

"But I want to."

"Well, you can't always have what you want."

"Yes, I can."

"We're not going fishing, they would fire me, then what would we eat?"

"Fish."

"Stop being so lazy. This is a very important day. You are going to meet a new friend. You won't have to live with me anymore."

"That's better than fishing. I like this day already."

"I thought you would."

"Jorge, people who talk to themselves are crazy. I think you are nuts."

"And I think you are right. Now go away."

With a laugh, Jorge walked over and stuffed the fat puppet into a shopping bag, then continued shaving.

A short time later, dressed in a t-shirt and jeans, Jorge Mendoza left his apartment building, a huge, dust-colored complex full of immigrant families with little children. As he walked down the steps, under his arm was the shopping bag with the puppet inside and a thick manila envelope.

Whistling a Christmas carol, he went to a battered pickup truck, unlocked the door and threw in the bag. Then he slid behind the wheel. The engine started, followed by a long squeal of belts. Before he put it into gear, he turned to a crucifix hanging from the mirror. Pulling it to his lips, he kissed it.

"Thank you, Jesus. You are so good to me. I do not deserve it."

Thirty minutes later, with a Christmas carol blaring from the radio, Jorge Mendoza's truck entered the employee parking lot at Children's Memorial Hospital. Pulling into a space at the back, he got out, taking the shopping bag with him.

Entering the main building, Jorge walked down a long corridor, nodding and smiling to people as he went. Everyone seemed to know him. Finally, he came to an employee locker room.

Going to his locker, he changed into the hospital scrubs of an orderly. Taped inside the door was the same picture of the dark, attractive woman holding the little girl. Jorge kissed it.

"Only one more week -- thank you, Jesus. We will have such a Christmas as there never was since God sent His son."

Closing the locker, he picked up the shopping bag and walked away.

Jorge's workday began and there were many important tasks to perform. He changed beds. He fed a child who couldn't move. He cleaned bathrooms on his hands and knees. And no matter what he did, he was whistling and happy.

In a private hospital room, a little girl sat in a huge bed. Balloons and cards were everywhere. A tiny Christmas tree was on a table. The child's forehead and eyes were heavily bandaged. A very tense young couple dressed in expensive clothes sat beside her.

Without being able to see them, the little girl turned in their direction. "Is the doctor coming?"

Her mother took her hand, "Yes, sweetheart. He's just very busy. There are lots of children in the hospital for him to see."

"I know."

Outside the child's room, Jorge was puttering around a hospital cart. A young surgeon walked briskly to the nursing station and checked a clipboard. He was about to enter the girl's room, when an older, kindly doctor in his sixties, stepped up and spoke in a low voice.

"Do you need any help with Ginny?"

"I don't think so, Bill. But thanks for asking."

"Okay. Well, I'm here if you need me." Clearly, the older man was concerned.

Patting him on the arm, the young surgeon entered Ginny's room. A nurse followed him. As Jorge worked at his cart, he exchanged a look with the doctor who remained in the hall.

"Good morning, Dr. Finnegan."

The older man just nodded.

As soon as the young surgeon entered the hospital room, the tension increased.

"Mr. and Mrs. Conlon, how is everyone?"

The little girl's mother tried to smile, "Fine, Dr. Stewart. How are you?"

"I'm well." He bent down. "And how are you feeling, Ginny?"

"Okay."

"Do your eyes hurt?"

"No, but I still see the sparkly things."

The nurse turned off the light and pulled the blinds.

"Well, let's get the bandages off and take a look at those beautiful eyes."

With the nurse assisting, he began removing the gauze.

"Okay, just one more piece. Now keep your eyes closed until I tell you to open them."

In the hall outside, Jorge continued puttering, trying not to make it obvious that he was watching what was happening in the room. Dr. Finnegan was doing the same thing. Slowly, the young surgeon peeled away the last of the bandages.

"Okay, Ginny, now open your eyes just a little bit. Everything might be blurry."

She obeyed. He held his hand in front of her face.

"Can you see my hand?"

"No."

Ginny's mother was biting her lip. Her father looked anguished.

"Can you see anything... like shadows or light?"

"No." She was growing frightened. "Just little sparkly things."

"Okay, that's all for now. Mr. Conlon, why don't you come out in the hall with me? Mrs. Conlon, maybe you could stay with Ginny."

The young mother nodded. She was crying, but she didn't make a sound for fear of frightening her daughter.

"Mommy?"

"I'm right here, sweetheart. It's okay. Everything's fine." She stroked her daughter's hair.

"Why can't I see anything?"

"I don't know, but we're going to find out. Don't worry."

The surgeon and Ginny's father stood in the hall not far from Jorge and Dr. Finnegan.

The young man was fighting back tears. "So, what does this mean, doctor?"

"I'm afraid it's not good."

"She's blind, isn't she?"

"We knew before the surgery that there was a fifty-fifty chance."

Ginny's father stared at the floor unable to speak.

"Of course, something could still happen, but I'm afraid it's unlikely. I'm very sorry. Why don't you go in and be with her. I'll come back in a little while."

The young father walked into the room. With tears in his eyes, he looked at his wife and shook his head.

"Mommy, where's daddy?"

"I'm right here, baby." He tried to make his voice sound natural, but couldn't quite do it. He sat down on the bed.

"Where's Dr. Stewart?"

"He's coming back in a while. He wants you to rest."

"Why can't I see anything but sparkles?"

The mother and father looked at each other. Both were crying silently. Her mother kissed her head.

"Let's not worry about that right now."

"I'm scared, Mommy."

Her mother held her.

Out in the hall, Dr. Finnegan was about to go into the room, when Jorge pulled the shopping bag from under the cart, walked to the door and knocked softly. The parents looked up.

"Excuse me, uhh, Mr. and Mrs. Conlon. I'm...a friend of Ginny's."

On hearing his voice, instantly the little girl smiled. "Jorge?"

"Hi, Ginny."

"Jorge cleans my room every day and makes everything smell good."

"I brought a little present, if it's all right?"

Her parents nodded. Jorge walked up to the bed.

"So, you got your bandages off. That's good. Now everybody can see how pretty you are. I've got something for you. It's a surprise and it's in a paper bag."

"What is it?"

Out of the bag, he pulled the fat furry puppet. Then Jorge spoke in the raspy puppet voice.

"I am so glad to be out of that bag. He keeps me there all the time. Hello, Ginny. Can you guess what I am?"

Jorge lifted her hand and helped her touch the fur.

"You're a furry puppet."

"You are right."

She ran her fingers over its face.

"You wear glasses." She hugged the puppet close. "What's his name?"

"I do not have a name. Lazy old Jorge forgot to give me one. I need a name. You can't go anyplace without a name."

"Ruffy. I'm gonna call you Ruffy."

"I like Ruffy. Ruffy is a very good name. From now on I am Ruffy."

Then, in his own voice Jorge said, "I think you should keep him. He doesn't like living with me."

"No, I do not like living with him. He makes me work hard all the time. Work. Work. Work. And I never get to play."

Ginny turned toward her mother, "Can I keep him, mommy?"

"Of course, sweetheart. But be sure to say thank you."

"Oh, thank you. I love him. He's my Ruffy."

The puppet hugged her. "And I love you too, Ginny. We will be very happy together."

Jorge stood up. "I'll come back later to see if he's being good."

As he left the room, Mrs. Conlon followed him into the hall.

With tears in her eyes she said, "I don't know how to thank you. The doctor doesn't think she'll ever see again."

Tears were in Jorge's eyes too. "I know. I am very sorry. I have been praying for her every day."

Please, keep praying...for all of us."

"I have a little girl too. She loves puppets, so I make them for her."

Mrs. Conlan looked back through the door at Ginny playing with Ruffy. "They're so wonderful."

Jorge pulled a small picture from his pocket. "This is my little girl."

"She's very pretty."

"Thank you. You have such a nice little girl, Mrs. Conlon. Don't be afraid. Jesus is with you and he can do anything."

"Thank you, I know he can."

Jorge smiled, then turned and pushed the cart away. At the nurse's station, Dr. Finnegan had seen it all.

CHAPTER FOUR

Wandering

Julie Gartman was so distraught that she couldn't stop shaking. She was sitting at the desk of a woman police sergeant.

"Ms. Gartman, there's really nothing more you can do. I'm sure we'll find your brother. Why don't you go home and get some rest?"

"That telephone number I gave you, it's a neighbor's house? Did I tell you that? I don't have a phone right now."

"Yes, you told me that."

"My mother passed away two weeks ago. We cut off her phone."

The sergeant replied gently, "You told me that too."

"I'm sorry. I'm not thinking very well."

"That's all right."

"I mean, he's been totally sheltered all his life. My mother did everything for him. I'm not even sure he knows his address. He was so upset this morning. If anything happens to him..."

"Ms. Gartman, his picture is out to all of our officers and it'll be on television and the Internet in an hour. We'll find him. Now, you go home. I'll call as soon as we have anything."

"Okay, thanks. I...guess that's what I'll do." Tears filled her eyes. Feeling a hundred years old, Julie got up and walked away.

Outside the police station, she went to her car. Then she stopped, buried her face in her hands and sobbed. "Oh, mom, I'm so sorry. I'm such a loser. I can't do anything right. How could someone like you have a daughter like me?"

Clutching his book and blanket, Eddie Gartman walked down a city street. He was enthralled with every sight and sound around him. Not far away, a man got out of a BMW, clicked on the alarm, and went into a store. Eddie was fascinated.

"Mr. Bunley-Mr. Bunley...Beep-beep. Beep-beep. Beep-beep. Beep-beep."

"Beeping" at the top of his lungs, he ran over, sat down on the hood of the BMW and began bouncing up and down. Instantly, the alarm shrieked with sixteen different tones and a mechanical voice blared out, "STEP BACK FROM THE VEHICLE. YOU HAVE BREACHED MY PERIMETER. STEP BACK IMMEDIATELY. THIS IS YOUR LAST WARNING."

Eddie was in heaven. "Beep-beep. Beep-beep. Beep-beep."

The BMW owner ran out of a store and yelled, "Hey, what are you doing? Get away from my car."

Screaming with laughter, Eddie ran, trailing the blanket like a streamer and yelling at the top of his lungs, "Beep-beep. Beep-beep. Beep-beep."

A few minutes later, out of breath, but still running and "beeping," he rounded a corner and came to a screeching halt. He was beside a freeway exit. Cars were speeding past.

Gasping for air, he mumbled, "Wait... wait... wait... wait... Mr. Bunley." Across from him stood an old man in a ratty suit, holding a Bible and a sign that read "Homeless tele-evangelist, will heal you for food. God bless you. (Also a Vietnam Vet)."

Suddenly, a Jaguar pulled up next to Eddie. The window rolled down and the driver waved a five dollar bill at him. Eddie just stared at it.

"Well, are you gonna take it or not?"

Eddie took it and the Jaguar sped away. He stared at the bill. Another car pulled up. Another five was thrust at him.

Eddie yelled excitedly, "Mr.-Bunley-Mr.Bunley. Money place. Money-money-money-money-money."

More cars stopped. Fives, ones, even half a sandwich were shoved into his hand. Grinning, Eddie stuck the sandwich in his mouth.

The homeless tele-evangelist stared malevolently at him. "Look, idiot, go find your own corner. This one's mine."

Chewing the sandwich and trying to keep from eating the money, which he held in the same hand, Eddie trudged off. Another block and he came to a city park. From somewhere in the distance, he heard the sound of a carousel.

"Wait. Listen-listen."

His eyes grew wide. Lifting the book, he stared at it, flipping pages until he came to one with a picture of Mr. Bunley on a carousel horse.

"Mr. Bunley-bump-bumpa-bump-bumpa-bumpa-bump--Come-on, come-on, come-on."

Eddie ran toward the music.

A carousel in the park was stopped to take on riders. A line of children and their parents were waiting. Puffing and out of breath, Eddie rushed straight to the front of the line and started to push through without paying.

The carousel operator grabbed him. "Hey, just a minute, pal. You got a lot of people ahead of you here."

"Gotta-get-on. Gotta-get-on. Gotta-get-on. Right-now-right-now-right-right-right-now.

The mother who was next in line nodded to man, "It's okay."

Rather sullenly, he mumbled, "All right, two-fifty. You got two-fifty?"

Eddie stared at him as though he were speaking another language.

"Money. You gotta have money to ride. Two dollars and fifty cents.

"Oh, money, money. Lots of money." Eddie shoved his whole wad of bills at the man.

"Okay, now wait a minute, just hang on."

But Eddie didn't wait. Running onto the carousel, he jumped on a horse. The operator followed him and stuffed the extra money back in his pocket. He barely noticed. He was too busy trying to make the horse move. A young mother started to put her child onto the horse next to his, but Eddie yelled, "No-no-no-no-no. No. NO. Sitting on

Mr. Bunley. Sitting-sitting-sitting. Off. Off. Off. Off."

Quickly, she found a different one. Finally, the carousel started turning. As it moved faster, Eddie was in heaven.

At the top of his voice he shrieked, "La, la-la-la-la-la-la-la-la. We're gonna find the-Singing-Place, the-Singing-Place. We're gonna find the Singing Place. Me-me-me and Mr. Buuunley."

CHAPTER FIVE

The End of Christmas

Jorge Mendoza was seated in the employee lunch room of the hospital, finishing a sandwich. A Christmas tree stood in the corner and a TV monitor on the wall was tuned to the news. Dr. Finnegan entered. Going to a machine, he bought a soft drink, then walked over to Jorge.

"Can I join you?"

Instantly, Jorge was self-conscious, "Of course, Dr. Finnegan."

With a slight groan, the older man lowered himself into a chair. "Did you know that Saint Francis of Assisi called his body Brother Ass? People would ask him how he was doing and he would say, 'Oh, I'm very well, but Brother Ass has seen better days.' That's me. Brother Ass has seen

better days. I hate getting old, Jorge. I don't rec-
ommend it to anyone. Your body starts doing
strange things. You sleep when you don't want to
and can't sleep when you do. And doctors, oh, my
God, stay away from those stupid idiots. They'll
kill you."

Jorge laughed.

Finnegan smiled, "Listen, I wanted to tell
you how much I appreciated the way you helped
Ginny Conlon and her parents this morning. You
did something that nobody else in this hospital
could have done."

Now Jorge was embarrassed, "Ginny is my
friend."

"It appears to me that you have quite a
number of friends around here. I see your puppets on every floor. It must take a lot of time to
make them."

"I like to do it. It keeps me busy."

"Look, if you need any material, my niece
owns a hobby and craft store. It's full of all kinds
of funny junk. And funny people too, if you ask
me. I'm sure I could get you a ton of scraps or almost anything else you might need."

"Oh, that would be wonderful. I always
need scraps. And foam for the heads."

"Well, you got a lot of people with foam
heads right here in this hospital. Just pull one off

and take it home. Nobody'll notice the difference. In a few days I'll bring you a trunk full of junk. How's that?"

"I will be so thankful."

"You know, I just had one of my many brilliant ideas, Jorge. Maybe you could put on a puppet show for the kids stuck here at Christmas. Let me tell you, this is a miserable place to open presents."

Jorge's eyes lit up. "Could I? I would love to do that. When my wife and daughter get here we could do it together. They are coming from Colombia. We could tell the Christmas story."

"Whether it's the Christmas Story or any other fairy tale, doesn't matter to me. Do whatever you want."

"The Christmas Story isn't a fairy tale, Dr. Finnegan."

"Yeah, yeah, fine, whatever. Just make'em laugh. That's all I care about. I'll set it up. So, how's everything going with immigration? I hear it's been a little rough."

Jorge was surprised, "You know about that?"

Finnegan laughed, "My friend, I've been here so long I know when somebody picks his nose in a restroom. Most of the time, I wish I didn't know any of it either. Stuff that goes on here makes a soap opera look tame. So how you been doin' with the paper pushing slugs who control our government?"

Jorge beamed, "We are finally finished. All the papers, mountains and mountains of papers. I have only one more meeting this afternoon. My wife and little girl have been accepted to come to the United States."

"Well, congratulations. Nice to hear something good actually got done in our worthless State Department. Look, if the hospital can do anything else to help you, I am a class "A" number one butt kicker. You just say the word and butts will go flying."

"Thank you, Dr. Finnegan. Everyone here has done so much already, a job for my wife, letters of recommendation. I am so thankful."

"All right. Well, let's plan on that Christmas puppet show."

"We will do a show like you have never seen. It will be like my grandparents used to do in Colombia. They were very famous. They traveled with a circus." Jorge looked at his watch. "I'm sorry, it's time for me to go. My last meeting with immigration is at four o'clock. "

"Well, you head on over there and kick a bureaucratic butt for me."

Beaming, Jorge got up and hurried from the room.

Suddenly, something on the television caught Finnegan's eye. It was a news alert delivered by a grim-faced anchor.

"Authorities are searching for 26-year-old Eddie Gartman who has been missing since ten o'clock this morning. Mr. Gartman is a special needs individual who is developmentally disabled."

Eddie's picture appeared on the screen.

"He was last seen on the embankment of the 101 freeway in the Silver Lake district. He is wearing a yellow shirt and jeans. If you have any information please call the police hotline-- (213) 555-5512. Needless to say, his family is very worried and we share their concern."

Carrying the manila envelope that he brought from home, Jorge Mendoza walked up the steps of an imposing government building. A sign in front read: U.S. CITIZENSHIP AND IMMIGRATION SERVICES--LOS ANGELES.

Moments later, he entered a large room filled with rows of desks where people of many nationalities sat talking to case workers. Making his way down the rows, he came to a particular desk where a pinch-faced, middle-aged man was seated at a computer. His name-plate read: MR. STONER. Jorge seemed confused.

The man looked up at him, "Can I help you, sir?"

"I'm looking for Mr. MacNamara."

"Mr. MacNamara is no longer with this office."

"But he was here a week ago. He has been handling my case."

"I've taken over his responsibilities. My name is Mr. Stoner. What can I do for you?"

Jorge pulled out a letter. "I got this in the mail. It said to come in at 4 o'clock today."

Stoner took the letter, read it, then turned to his computer and began punching in numbers.

"Please, sit down."

Jorge sat.

"You are...Jorge Mendoza?

"Yes."

"And your wife's name is Ana?"

"That's right and our daughter is Maria."

Stoner scanned screen after screen of information.

Suddenly, Jorge felt very nervous. "Mr. MacNamara told me everything was ready. My wife and daughter will come in a few days."

There was no response.

"I have copies of all their papers." He held up the envelope.

"Please be patient, Mr. Mendoza. There's a flag on your file."

Jorge turned pale. "A flag? What does that mean, a flag?"

"I don't know. I'm checking."

"My wife and daughter already have their tickets. We've waited over three years. I brought the file with me--letters of support, an offer of employment from the hospital where I work, birth certificates, our marriage certificate. She has been interviewed at the U.S. Consulate in Barranquilla and they've both passed their medical examinations. Mr. MacNamara said we were all finished."

Stoner turned away from the computer and stared at him over his reading glasses. "The filing process is complete. But, I'm afraid I have bad news. Your wife has been denied entry into the United States."

Jorge was so stunned, he could barely speak. "What? But...why?"

"Our investigators have concluded that she is a security risk."

"A security risk? There must be a mistake. Do you have the right name? This is Ana Mendoza."

"I have the correct file. Unfortunately, the Department of Homeland Security has determined that your wife is a member of an organization with very dangerous affiliations."

"That cannot be. My wife is not a member of an organization. She is...she is...my wife."

"According to the investigation, she belongs to the Little Sisters of the Sacred Heart."

"But that's only a women's group of the church. They help orphans. They go into the countryside and bring food and clothes to the poor. They do good things. Wonderful things. This is a mistake."

Stoner's eyes narrowed, "Apparently, that's not all they do, Mr. Mendoza. Their activities aide and abet the terrorist and drug activities of the Sanchez Cartel."

"No. No, no. No cartels. All they do is help people who are hungry--who don't have any clothes. They don't have anything to do with drugs."

Stoner turned away, "In any case, I didn't make this determination. I'm only informing you of it. And the decision is final. Your wife cannot enter the United States."

Suddenly, Jorge was struggling for air. "But...she is...a good woman. She... loves people. She makes...puppets for poor children. That's all.

I swear. Please... do not do this to us. We have waited...so long...and worked so hard."

"It's out of my hands, Mr. Mendoza. Of course, you do have the right to appeal."

"But that could take years."

"Quite true. And given her...record, I doubt that you would be successful."

"Her record? Her record of what, making puppets? What am I going to tell her? What am I going to tell our little girl? They were coming for Christmas."

"I'm sorry. All I can say is that your case is closed." He went back to his computer.

Utterly overwhelmed, Jorge stared at him. Slowly, his eyes filled with tears, which he tried to blink away. Finally, clutching the envelope, he got up and walked back through the rows of desks. For the first time, he looked like an old man.

It was evening.

Once more, Jorge Mendoza stood at his hospital locker. He was emptying it, dropping the contents piece by piece, into a garbage bag. As the pieces fell, he mumbled a song in Spanish and took hits from a bottle of tequila. Finally, all that was left was the picture. This he carefully peeled off the door. After looking at it, he stuck it in his pocket, then picked up the bag and walked away.

Singing, with the garbage bag slung over his shoulder, Jorge made his way down the main hospital corridor toward the door.

Dr. Finnegan came out of an office. "Jorge...?"

Jorge stopped and turned. When he saw the doctor, he grinned, "Feliz Navidad, Dr. Finnegan, Feliz Navidad." Then he continued walking.

Finnegan caught up with him. "Jorge, are you all right?"

"I am very, very fine. I am so wonderful. That is me." He started singing again.

"What's happened?"

"What...has...happened? You want to know what has happened? I will tell you what has happened. No Christmas puppet show. That is what has happened. Cancelled. Gone."

"But why?"

"Because I cannot do it alone. Only two arms. Need four. Don't have them, so...all over."

"What about your wife?"

"Not coming."

"What?"

Jorge stopped, grinned broadly and bent close. "You want to hear a very funny joke? You want to know why she is not coming? They say she is a very dangerous person. My wife, Ana Mendoza. They do not want her in your country.

But they are lying. She is only a good woman who helps the poor, and for this they have turned her away. Merry Christmas, Dr. Finnegan. Feliz Navidad."

Still singing, Jorge walked out of the hospital. Too stunned to speak, Finnegan stared after him.

CHAPTER SIX

The Storm

William Finnegan entered the human resources department of Children's Hospital. Half a dozen people were busy at desks. He went straight to a particular desk where an attractive, middle-aged woman was seated. Dropping into a chair in front of her, he bent close and spoke low.

"Joan, has Jorge Mendoza been in here today?"

"Yes, just a little while ago."

"What happened?"

"He quit."

"Did he say why?"

"He didn't talk to me, but I overheard. He just said he was finished and wasn't coming back. Pam tried to arrange an exit interview, but he refused. All he did was give an address for his last check." She paused. It was clear there was something more.

"Come on, Joan, what is it?"

Glancing around, she spoke very quietly, "Well, he'd been drinking."

"Could I see his personnel file?"

"Doctor, you know I can't do that. I could get into a lot of trouble."

"You saw him. Something bad has happened. The man needs help."

She hesitated.

"I've got two Lakers tickets for you."

"Are you trying to bribe me, Dr. Finnegan?"

"Only if it'll work."

"There's no need. I'm worried about Jorge too. He's such a nice man." She wrote something on a post-it note. "Go to your office computer. Here's the password for his HR file. Don't print anything out and don't stay on too long."

"I'm gonna give you those tickets anyway."

"You'd better."

"Hey, I just had one of my many brilliant ideas. Let me take you to the game."

She smiled, "We'll see."

Distant lightning flashed over black water. A powerful offshore wind was blowing in from the ocean, bending palm trees and sending billows of filth into the air. A huge winter storm lashed the waves as it streaked out of the darkness of the Pacific toward the City of the Angels.

Lying on his cot in his apartment, Jorge Mendoza barely noticed the thunder. He was singing a bawdy song in Spanish and taking long slugs of tequila.

Suddenly, there was a crack and a roar that shook the whole building. The singing stopped and Jorge stared at the ceiling.

With slurred words he called out, "So, God, is that you? Rumble, rumble, rumble. You angry like Jorge, maybe? I don't think so. People think you are up there. Me? I'm not so sure. You let bad things happen to a good woman like Ana. And to a little girl. Always, I thought you love children."

He took a long suck on the bottle.

"I tell you what I think, God. I think maybe you don't care so much. Too big. Too far away. We pray and pray and it don't mean nothing. How 'bout we make a deal? You don't care, I don't care. And I don't pray no more to you. How 'bout that? You like that deal? So, tomorrow, I will call Ana and break her heart."

Picking up the photograph of his wife and daughter, he started crying.

"You see, Ana? You see what helping people does? You always say to me, 'Help people. Be kind to people. Do good and Jesus will bless you.' So, I help, I am kind and it don't matter. You cannot come. They won't let you. It's just me, all by myself, with this big damn bunch of ugly puppets."

He stared around the room. Suddenly, the puppets were everywhere. They covered the walls, the ceiling, the floor, the stove and the table. Their faces were larger than before and they were leering at him, grinning and laughing.

"So you laugh at Jorge. Go ahead and laugh. Laugh at the stupid man. You want to laugh? I will teach you to laugh."

Pulling out a garbage bag, he began stumbling around the room, stuffing puppets into it. He grabbed them from everywhere, cursing each one, until the room was empty and the bag would barely close. Then, dragging it behind him, he rushed out of the apartment.

The wind was blowing much harder and rain was falling as Jorge staggered down the front steps of his building and over to his truck. Before he could get to it, there was a downpour and he was drenched.

Cursing and wiping the water out of his eyes, he threw the bag into the back and fumbled for his keys. By the time he had unlocked the door and slid behind the wheel, he looked like a drowned rat. But the water sobered him a little.

He saw the crucifix hanging on the mirror. Jerking it off, he held it up and yelled, "Five years I work. Five years. I pay for my nephew's school. My sister's medicine. My mother's funeral. My family's food. I try to save money. Only once a year do I see my little girl. Once a year! But you don't care. You don't care about nothing."

Starting the engine, he pulled out, almost hitting a parked car as he swung into the street and drove off.

Forty minutes later, with rain falling in sweeping sheets and thunder crashing, Jorge's truck swerved into an empty parking lot at a beach.

Throwing open the door, he dragged the bag of puppets from the back and stumbled out onto a long pier. When he reached the end, he opened the bag and began throwing puppets into the ocean.

With each one, he cursed and yelled, "Here, this is for you, God. And this one. And this one.

You take everything from me. So you can have these too. She was only helping people. Praying for people. You don't care nothing for us."

Finally, the bag was empty. Dozens of puppet heads floated in the black, raging water beneath the pier. Jorge reached into his pocket and pulled out the crucifix.

Above the storm he yelled, "So, Jesus, I always believe in you. I believe you died to save us from our sins. I believe you are God and you love us. I believe if I pray you hear me. I think you give me the puppets. I think you tell me how to make them. And I do it. I give them to children. I pray for the children, but nothing happens. They stay blind. They can't walk. They just die. And now this happen to my little girl. So I don't believe in you anymore. Goodbye to you, Jesus."

With all his strength, he threw the crucifix out into the darkness. Then he huddled against the rail, soaked and weeping.

Jorge was about to turn and go, when he heard an odd sound.

Gradually, it grew louder.

Above the roaring wind and waves, he thought he heard singing. Puzzled, he looked out over the ocean...and his eyes grew wide.

Far away, in the black sky, strange lights were swirling. They danced in undulating shafts, floating and weaving in the raging storm and twisting through them were veins of lightning.

Suddenly, the singing was much louder. Jorge didn't just hear it, he felt it in his body. It sang in his flesh and bones. It sang in the wood of the pier. It sang in the drops of rain and the crashing waves. It sang like ten thousand angels joined in a chant of overwhelming majesty and terrifying power.

And in that singing, over and over, he heard a Voice calling his name.

As Jorge stood trembling, the dancing light rushed toward him. Before he could move, it was directly overhead. Then it began to descend.

Frightened out of his mind, Jorge ran toward beach. But he got only a few feet before he slipped and fell. Instantly, the pier was covered with millions of tiny falling stars. Like rain, they dropped around him, bursting into silvery splashes that sang with the music of Heaven.

Choked with terror, Jorge looked up. Above him hung a Pillar of Brilliance far greater than all the rest. For a moment, it remained suspended. Then, as the singing rose to a great crescendo, like a white-hot avalanche, it roared straight down.

The pier disintegrated into burning shards and Jorge dropped into the ocean. As he sank in the black water, his face turned upward.

Just above the surface drifted the great Pillar of Light. In it, was a Hand so filled with glory that it burned his eyes. From between closed fingers flowed streaks of living fire. Sweeping down into the ocean, the hand opened. The palm was pierced with crimson brilliance that flowed like blood.

Drowning, Jorge reached toward it.

And the Hand grasped his.

There was a flash that turned the black ocean into burning day...and then everything went dark.

Rain continued to fall. The wind howled and waves crashed onto the sand. Over the glistening surf rode the puppet faces, staring up into an empty sky.

Jorge Mendoza lay on his back in the sand, half in the water. Strewn around him in the moonlight were dozens of puppets. Each time the surf swept in, his legs rose and fell with it. He didn't move. His eyes were open, staring at nothing. His clothes were soaked and scorched. An empty tequila bottle lay beside him.

In the darkness, there was the sound of an engine. Then, headlights appeared. A truck stopped and shadowy figures got out. It was the beach patrol.

"Aw, crap, another floater. I hate floaters." It was a man's voice.

Another man replied, "Maybe he was on the pier. Look at all puppets. Where the heck did they come from?"

One of them pushed Jorge with a boot. Jorge groaned.

"Well, wherever he was, he was suckin' down the hooch." He kicked the bottle. "Hey, wake up, pal. No sleepin' on the beach. Get your butt out of here or we'll run you in. You hear me? Come on, get up, get going."

Jorge struggled to his hands and knees. Then, he puked, gagging out sea water.

"That's right, get it out. Then *get out.*"

Finally, he managed to wobble to his feet. His head was splitting and his eyes wouldn't focus. Slowly, he looked around. The men were like shimmering ghosts in the headlights of the truck.

"Come on, move."

He staggered across the sand to the parking lot. Opening the door of his truck, Jorge half fell inside. Dizzy and ill, he pulled himself into a sitting position and leaned against the wheel.

Then, he saw something that almost made him pass out again. The crucifix he had thrown in the ocean was hanging back on the mirror.

"What...?"

He touched it, not sure it was real. The instant he did so, he heard an odd crackling sound like fire in dry grass. His hand was tingling.

Slowly, he turned it over. Tiny streaks of light flickered across his skin and a drop of crimson shimmered in his palm.

He yelled. Instantly, the vision disappeared and his hand looked normal.

"I'm sick. I've got to get home." But he didn't feel drunk anymore.

The keys were still in the ignition. Jorge started the engine, threw the pickup into gear and drove away.

CHAPTER SEVEN

Danger

An exhausted and soaked Eddie Gartman dragged his way down a sleazy Los Angeles boulevard. The garish lights of porno shops and topless clubs reflected in pools of oil-streaked water. Prostitutes, emerging after the storm, approached him. But when they saw his face, they quickly moved away.

Suddenly, a couple of gang bangers stepped out from the shadows of a building.

"Hey, dog."

Eddie stared at them, "Dog? Dog-dog."

They started laughing. "Well, look what we got. We got us a cracker retard. Who let you out, fool?"

"Dog? Dog-dog."

"Yeah, you a dog."

Surrounding him, they moved in close. Eddie was confused.

"Dog? Dog, dog?"

"You know how to bark like a dog? Well, do it. Go ahead, bark like a dog, retard."

Eddie stared at them. Finally, he whispered, "Dog?"

"He too stupid to bark like a dog. Look at him, don't got no brains at all. How much money you got, fool?"

"Dog-dog?"

"Don't say that no more. Don't want to hear no more "dog-dog." I said how much money you got? You too stupid to know? Then we better take a look."

Shaking him down, they pulled out what was left of the wad of bills.

"This is it? This is all you got? Bring dog-dog inside."

One of them grabbed Eddie by his mop of hair. With a yell, he pulled away and ran.

"Get him!"

But he was surprisingly fast. Yelling, "dog, dog, dog, dog," he streaked off, with the blanket flapping.

A block away, he turned down a dark alley. Instantly, he was flopping and wallowing over piles on the ground. The alley was strewn with sleeping bums lying under old tarps and boxes. As he stumbled over them, yelling, "dog, dog, dog," the men cursed him. And the gang was right behind.

But the chase only went a few more feet. The alley ended in a brick wall. When the gang caught him, one of them grabbed him around the neck from behind, "Where you goin', fool?"

Eddie started choking.

"Gimme that blanket."

"No. No-no-no..."

The gangster grabbed it.

"No!" With all his strength, Eddie pulled away. They both kept pulling on the blanket until Eddie tripped and fell. Then the gang kicked him until he let loose.

A skinny kid covered with tattoos bent down. "You stupid little pig-for- brains, gimme that book."

"No-no. Please-please, Mr. Bunley." Eddie clutched it to his chest.

The gang started kicking him again. Finally, the book was torn away. Eddie lay with his cheek cut, sobbing, "Mommy, mommy, mommy."

The tattooed gangster stared at the book cover. "What it say?" He shoved it at one of the bums who was cowering next to a dumpster. "I said, what it say?"

"It say, Mr. Bunley's Happy Singing Place."

They all jeered. Bored with the game, they tossed the book and blanket into the garbage bin.

"We need to put this fool in a Happy Singing Place."

They picked up Eddie. As he yelled and struggled, they shoved him head-first into the reeking dumpster. Laughing, they slammed the lid and walked away.

In the darkness and filth, Eddie sobbed. Finally, he pushed open the lid and peeked out.

One of the bums mumbled, "They gone, dirty little jerks. You okay?"

Eddie didn't answer. Clutching his book and blanket, he climbed out of the bin and ran.

Twenty minutes later, exhausted and sobbing, he stumbled down a deserted street lined with warehouses. "Mommy-mommy-mommy-mommy. Mr. Bunley. Where-where...?"

He was so tired that he could barely walk. Not far away, a loading dock jutted out from a building. Hobbling over to it, he found a hole leading underneath. Crouching down, he crawled inside.

Eddie sat in the dark trembling, clutching his book and blanket and whispering, "Mommy...."

Feeling something in his pocket, he pulled out the tiny Christmas ornament. Holding it close, he covered his head with the blanket and lay down.

CHAPTER EIGHT

Angel Vultures

Jorge Mendoza drove through the streets of Los Angeles as though all hell were after him. His clothes were scorched and torn and he reeked of polluted sea water. Sweat poured down his face. Mumbling, he kept shifting his gaze to the crucifix.

Then, slowly, a new terror began. He started hearing voices. At first he wasn't sure, but, as he strained to listen, they got louder – soft, ghostly whispers in a language that he couldn't understand.

"Oh God, oh God, what is happening to me? I am going crazy."

He rubbed his eyes.

"What is *this?*"

Around him, the city was changing. The lights in the buildings began to glow with an unearthly brightness, while everything else was growing very dark. Heavy mist appeared, making it almost impossible to see ahead.

Suddenly, something huge and black streaked down in front of his truck. Jorge yelled and slammed on his brakes. But as fast as it had come, it was lost in the fog. Was it a giant bird? It had looked like a bird, but its wings were far larger than any bird that Jorge had ever seen.

He thought he heard a scream, but nothing was visible. A moment later, another one flashed in front of him. He hunched over, trying to look up at the sky through his windshield. What he saw froze him.

High above, hundreds of black creatures with huge wings soared between the buildings. Silently, one after another swooped down into the thick mist.

There was another scream.

A woman's scream.

Soon anguished wails came from everywhere.

And the things weren't just swooping to the street. Some were flying straight into buildings. They would wheel and vanish through a wall as though it were made of smoke. v

The fog parted. Dozens of people were passing on the sidewalks and above most of them floated black-winged creatures. Like parasites, they were attached. At the end of long arms were vicious talons, which were sunk into every person's back.

As Jorge watched, one of the monsters swooped onto a man. With huge claws it struck him, tearing open a fearful gash in his head. The man cried out, but kept on walking as though nothing had happened. Then the thing embedded itself in his flesh.

What were they? Where had they come from? Into Jorge's mind came two words – Angel Vultures.

Their attacks didn't stop. Over and over, the black wings streaked down. After tearing hideous wounds, they would attach to their victim. Many of the people would writhe in agony, but they didn't seem to know what was causing their pain. They just kept walking.

Suddenly, one of them landed on Jorge's roof. Talons came straight through the steel. But as they groped for him, they touched the crucifix. There was a crimson flash. With a gagging croak, the thing pulled back and flew away.

As quickly as the hideous vision had come, it faded. The darkness brightened. The fog disappeared and the black creatures with it. The city looked normal once more.

"Oh God, oh God, oh God, what have you done to me?"

Jorge careened around a corner. Children's Hospital was ahead. He didn't even bother going to the parking lot. Screeching to a stop at the curb, he jumped out and ran toward the entrance. But before he got there, once more, he heard the cries and wailing. He turned to look.

Los Angeles was engulfed in black flames darker than the darkest night. The raging inferno seemed to rise to the stars. In the sky, Jorge saw thousands and thousands of the winged creatures soaring and swooping. And from the City of the Angels came a great, anguished cry.

Almost out of his mind with terror, Jorge rushed into the lobby of the hospital. Once inside, he saw people, but they were like ghosts moving in slow motion. And none of them saw him.

He rushed to the front desk where a woman was seated. "Please, I need help. I got hit by lightning."

There was no response. It was as though he wasn't even there.

"Don't you hear me? I need help. Look at me."

But she didn't look. She just kept shuffling papers.

Down the hall, he saw a doctor that he knew and ran up to her.

"Dr. Anderson, you've got to help me. I've been hurt." He tried to grab her arm, but his hand passed straight through. He stared in horror.

"I know what this is. I am dead. I don't have a body anymore. I am dead and this is hell. Oh, Jesus, forgive me. I didn't mean what I said. Please, don't leave me here."

As though in a nightmare, Jorge wandered down one corridor after another.

"I am dead and what will happen to my wife and little girl? What will happen to my family? I am the one who helps them. I send them money so they can have food, so they can go to doctors. Please, God, they are very poor. Please take me out of hell and I will never get drunk again. I will never say bad things again."

Suddenly, he froze.

Ahead in the corridor was shimmering brightness. Slowly, it formed into the Pillar of Light that had been over the ocean. And then, he heard singing.

Jorge turned to run, but something grasped his shoulder and spun him around. No one was there.

Slowly, the Light moved into a hospital room. In his mind, Jorge heard a soft voice say, "Come and see."

Shaking so hard, he could barely walk, Jorge went to the door and looked in.

It was Ginny's room. The little girl lay asleep on the bed. The ugly puppet he had given her was in her arms. Her mother was sleeping on a cot beside her.

Then something else became visible. Near the ceiling, above the bed, in steaming mist, hung one of the hideous black creatures. Its outstretched wings filled the top of the room. Never had Jorge seen a face so vile. The head was shaped like a huge axe with eyes set wide apart. It had no mouth, but twin serpent tongues flickered in and out from two holes where a mouth should have been.

One of its long arms was hanging down and its talons were buried in the little girl's chest. The other arm dangled to her mother's breast where the talons pierced her heart. The thing didn't move. On its face was a strange look.

What was that look?

It was ecstasy.

The eyes were closed and the face contorted in an endless orgasm of hellish ecstasy.

Instantly, Jorge knew what it was doing. The ecstasy came because it was sucking life from Ginny and her mother. And in the place of life, it was poisoning them with the deepest fear and anguish.

Suddenly, Jorge was filled with a hate so deep that he could barely hold it in. In a teeth-gritting rage, he entered the room.

Once more, he heard the crackle of fire likes flames in dry grass...and lifted his hand. Light rippled over his fingers. A shimmering drop of crimson appeared in his palm that was so bright he couldn't look at it.

He walked up to the bed. Lost in its vile pleasure, the creature didn't seem aware of him. Slowly, he reached out and grasped the arm that was attached to the little girl.

Huge black eyes flashed open. Then from the monster came a shriek that shook the room. With a croak of agony, it pulled its talons from the mother and child and went up in flames that were more like acid than fire. As its wings, its head, its body, were engulfed, it writhed and from it spewed black bile that reeked of the purest hate.

In a moment, all of it was gone.

Jorge looked down at Ginny. Neither she nor her mother had awakened. He looked at his hand. It was covered with blood so drenched with brilliance that he was almost blinded. Jorge never understood why he did what he did next. Bending over the little girl, he touched her closed eyes with his bloody fingers and whispered her name.

Instantly, she began to awaken.

"Mommy?"

Her mother stirred.

Realizing what he had done, Jorge was terrified. He rushed from the room.

"What's the matter, honey?"

Ginny sat up.

"Mommy?"

Drenched with sweat, Jorge ran down the hall. Suddenly, he was dizzy. Stumbling into a restroom, he grabbed his face, crying out in pain.

The room was filled with blood-red shadows and everything was growing dim. Going to a mirror, he stared at himself. From his eyes, ran drops of blood.

"Oh, God...oh, God..."

Images began appearing, vivid memories that were not his own.

Brilliant sunshine falling through trees.

Laughing.

Sitting on a swing.

Going back and forth...higher and higher.

The laughing voice belonged to a little girl.

The memory changed.

In front of him was a living room. How large it was. A man entered, smiling. The man bent down.

Running toward him.

Running like a child.

Strong arms reached down. He was lifted into the air.

Then it was gone.

The room was gone.

Riding now.

Riding in a car.

A crash.

Stretchers.

People yelling.

Blood-red vision.

Then flashing lights and awful sounds.

Ginny's voice echoed, "Mommy? Mommy, where are you? I can't see..."

The images faded.

The restroom was growing darker as Jorge whispered the same words, "I can't see."

He stumbled into the hall. Everything was a blur. The ghost-people in the corridor took no notice of him. They were rushing toward Ginny's room.

Staggering to an elevator, Jorge groped for the buttons. Then, everything went pitch black.

"Somebody help me!"

The doors opened. He fell through onto his knees. The doors closed. He groped the wall for the buttons. Finally, he touched one.

The elevator dropped. The door opened. He staggered out yelling, "Help! Help!"

He was in a deserted basement storage room. Plunging down a corridor of shelves, he knocked over boxes and equipment.

"Somebody help me. I'm blind."

Deeper and deeper into the room, he stumbled. Suddenly, he hit a shelf full of huge boxes. With a tremendous crash, the whole thing came down on him and he fell, unconscious, to the floor.

CHAPTER NINE

Breakfast and Regrets

Morning sunlight flooded the loading dock where Eddie Gartman was hiding. He wasn't visible, but from under the dock his voice could be heard having an argument.

"No-no-no-no-no-no. Not listening-not-listening-not-listening. NO."

In cobwebbed shadows strewn with trash, Eddie sat in a disheveled heap clutching his blanket and book and arguing with the imaginary Mr. Bunley.

"Not-going-not-going. Not-not-not-not-not. Mad-at-Mr.Bunley. Mad-mad-mad. No-Singing-Place. Scary-place-and-scary-place-and-scary-place. Not going. Staying-staying. Hungry. HUNGRY."

Suddenly, a door next to the dock opened. Eddie perked up his ears and whispered, "Shhh, no, no talking."

Two workmen emerged from the building carrying steaming McDonald's breakfasts in styrofoam containers.

The older man was about to sit down, when he remembered something. "You got the manifests?"

His partner groaned, "I left'em upstairs."

"Better go get'em. Truck could get here any minute."

"Yeah, yeah, all right."

"While you're doin' that, I'm gonna hit the john." Carrying his breakfast, he headed back toward the building. The younger man set his food on the dock.

"Wouldn't leave it there if I was you."

"Why not? I'll only be gone a minute. I've spilled it once already."

"Suit yourself."

When the door closed behind them, Eddie's head popped out. He stared at the breakfast container and smiled.

"I'm lovin' it. I'm lovin' it."

A few minutes later, the workmen returned.

"Hey, where's my food?"

"Told ya."

"You gotta be kidding me. Somebody swiped my food."

"Got a lot o' bums around here."

"I'm gonna find whoever did this and kick their ass."

While the older man sat down to eat, the younger one stalked up and down the alley yelling, "Come out right now. You hear me? I know you're still here. Give me back my food. I'm gonna kick your ass."

"Gotta say that's not much of an invitation. Give back breakfast and get your ass kicked all in one morning. Not somethin' I'd jump at. You can have one of my pancakes."

"I don't want one of your pancakes. I want my pancakes."

"Suit yourself." He took a huge buttery bite.

Three blocks away, Eddie was scrunched between a wall and a dumpster stuffing pancakes and sausage into his mouth. While he ate, he mumbled, "Lots, lots, lots for me, but none, none, none, for Mr. Buuuunley."

Julie Gartman's neighbor, Rose, was behind the wheel of her car driving down a quiet street. Julie sat exhausted in the passenger seat with her head against the window.

Rose looked over at her. "Well, honey, what do you think?"

"I think we've been driving around all night and I'm wasting your time. We need to go home. That's what I think."

"Don't worry about my time. I've got plenty of that, but I'm not sure I can keep my eyes open much longer."

"This is stupid. I don't know why I ever thought we could find him."

The older woman patted her shoulder, "We had to try, Sweetie."

"If he dies, I'll never forgive myself."

"Julie, stop talkin' like that. He's not going to die. Somebody'll find him. And I'll bet it'll be soon."

"Yeah, they'll find him – dead beside a freeway."

"Don't think such terrible thoughts. We've got to have faith in God. He hasn't forgotten your little brother. He knows exactly where he is and He's taking care of him."

"You sound like my mother." Julie's voice grew quiet and bitter. "No matter what kind of crap happened, she never stopped believing in Jesus. Garbage could be falling all over us and she'd still head off to church. Well, that's not me. I gave up on all that God stuff a long time ago. If there's a

God, he wouldn't have let my father walk out on us. Just packed up and left and we never saw him again. For years, my mom worked two miserable jobs, while I took care of Eddie. "

"I know."

"Yeah, of course, you do. You and your family helped us so much. I don't know what we would've done if you hadn't been there."

"God helps us by using the hands of people, Julie."

"Yeah, well, the only hands I ever saw were yours. The sad thing is my mother never stopped loving that sperm donor."

"Don't call him that, Julie. He's still your father."

"No, he isn't. I don't have a father. My mother may have forgiven that jerk, but I never will. Even though she never saw him again, she was praying for him the day she died."

"Your mother was a wonderful woman." Rose paused searching for words. "Julie, I've lived a long time and I've learned a few things. There's a reason for all the pain in the world. The way things are right now isn't the way God wants them to be. And they won't be this way forever. That's in the Bible."

"There's a lot in the Bible that I don't believe." Tears filled Julie's eyes. "If there's a God, why would he let my brother be born the way he is? I know why my father left. He just couldn't handle Eddie. And you know what's so horrible? I know exactly how he felt. When I was a teenager, I wanted Eddie to go away and never come back. Sometimes I even wanted him to die."

Rose shook her head, "Now, that isn't true and I know it. I watched you for too long. You've always loved Eddie."

"You're right. From the moment they brought him home I loved him. Born on Christmas day. What a gift. Everything just turned into craziness."

She stared out the window.

"You know what was worst about growing up with Eddie? Going into restaurants. Everyone would be talking and laughing and then we'd walk in. It would get quiet. People would look at him and then straight at me – like we were both freaks. After that, they'd stare and stare until I wanted to scream. Thankfully, we didn't go to restaurants very often. Couldn't afford it."

Her eyes grew soft.

"Oh, but, when he was a baby he was so beautiful. Sometimes I thought I was holding an angel. He'd sit on my lap for hours, smiling up at me. And he never stopped smiling...until the day our mother died."

The tears were running down her cheeks.

"I'll never forget Eddie at her funeral. He loved her more than anything, but when he looked at her in the casket, he never said a word...and he never cried. Not a single tear. It was like being there alone. No father. No mother. No brother. I was so lonely. You want to believe in God? That's fine, but it's not for me." She cried softly. "I'm so sorry, Rose. You drive around all night with me, then I sit here and bitch."

"There's nothing to apologize for, honey."

"I'm just so tired. You know what I'd like to do?"

"What's that?"

"I'd like to lie down and go to sleep forever."

Rose stroked her hair. "God knows all about your broken heart, Julie. I'm praying to Him for a miracle. And you want to know something? I think you're going to get one."

CHAPTER TEN

A Slight Problem

Jorge Mendoza groaned. He was lying under the pile of boxes in the storage room. Slowly, he pulled himself out and stared around. Then he remembered...and touched his eyes.

"What happened to me?"

Struggling to his feet, he teetered with dizziness. His head ached. He looked down at his clothes. They were scorched and torn.

"Oh God...that part wasn't a dream."

Going to the elevator, he pushed the button. The door opened and he got inside. He pushed another button. As it started to rise, he groaned and leaned against a wall. He felt miserable.

Moments later, he stepped out into a busy hospital corridor. People stared at his clothes. An orderly pushing a cart stopped.

"Dude, what happened to you?"

"A bad night."

"No kidding."

Jorge kept walking...straight to Ginny's room. He looked inside. It was empty. A nurse came up.

"Can I help you?" Then she saw who it was. "Jorge?"

"Where's Ginny?"

"Upstairs in ophthalmology. You look awful. What happened to your clothes?"

"It is a long story. I've got to see her."

"I don't think that's possible."

"Why not?"

"Look, something weird happened last night. We're not supposed to talk about it. Were you in a fire?"

"She's all right, isn't she?"

"Yeah, she's fine. Better than fine."

"What do you mean?"

Her voice dropped to a whisper, "Okay, just don't tell anybody where you heard it. The doctors are really freaked out. During the night, Ginny woke up...and she wasn't blind anymore."

"What?"

"She could see perfectly. And the story she's telling is making everybody crazy."

"What kind of story?"

"That somebody came in the middle of the night and touched her eyes. From that moment, she started seeing."

Jorge was trembling. He turned and walked away.

"Jorge?"

He ran to the stairs.

After climbing four flights, he left the stairwell and ran down a hall to a door marked "Ophthalmology." Very cautiously, he pushed it open and looked inside. Not seeing anyone, he entered.

Jorge was in a lab filled with equipment. At first, it appeared to be deserted. But, then, he heard voices coming from the back. Quietly, he found a place where he could see without being seen.

Ginny was sitting on an examination table. Her parents were with her. Dr. Stewart and several other physicians were completing an examination.

Stewart turned to the Conlans. "Well, I can't explain it, but her eyes are perfect. There's not even any evidence of my surgery."

The Conlans were in tears. "Thank God, oh, thank God."

Stewart bent down to the little girl, "Ginny, why don't you tell, Dr. Feinberg and Dr. Blake what you told me."

"Okay." She took a deep breath, "I was asleep. Then it felt like somebody touched my eyes and everything popped."

Dr. Feinberg frowned, "Popped?"

Stewart interjected, "I think she means flashed."

Ginny nodded, "A really big flash."

"And that's when you called your mother?"

"Uh huh."

Dr. Blake turned to Mrs. Conlon. "You didn't see anything?"

"No. And I woke up right away. We were the only ones in the room, but there was a strange burned smell. From that moment, she started seeing again."

Ginny raised her hand. "Wait. I just remembered something."

"What is it?"

"He said my name."

"Who?"

"The man who touched my eyes."

"So it was a man?" Dr. Stewart looked at his colleagues.

"Yes, and he said, 'Ginny'."

Jorge felt like throwing up. Quickly, he slipped out of the room, then went to an elevator. The door slid open and Dr. Finnegan stepped out. But that was the last person he wanted to see.

"Jorge!"

Jorge ran for the stairs.

"Jorge, wait." Finnegan ran after him.

Minutes later, the front door of the hospital burst open. Jorge raced to his truck, jumped in and drove off, just as Finnegan came running out after him.

The doctor watched the truck disappear around a corner. Folding his arms, he smiled a tight-lipped smile. "You think you can run away from me, Mr. Mendoza? You don't know who you're dealing with." He turned and walked back into the building.

A short time later, Jorge pulled to a stop in front of a small Roman Catholic Church. Jumping out, he rushed inside.

A light was on over a confessional and he headed straight for it. Stepping in, he closed the door.

Sweating and breathing hard, Jorge stared at the screen. Through it, he could see the vague form of a priest.

Words came pouring out, "Bless-me-Father-for-I-have-sinned.   It's-been-a-month-since-my-last-confession-and-I-am-in-a-lot-of-trouble."

"What's your trouble, my son?"

"God is after me and you've got to help me get away."

"And why would He be after you?"

"I think I did something very, very stupid."

"What was that?"

"I threw some puppets in the ocean and then I threw in a crucifix."

"You threw what in the ocean?"

"Puppets and a crucifix."

"Why did you do that?"

"The puppets started looking at me funny and I got angry. But this isn't about them. It's about the crucifix. I think that's my big problem."

"Why did you throw it in the ocean?"

"I got angry at God too."

"So the puppets and God made you angry."

"Yes, also, I was very drunk."

"Well that might explain a little bit."

"No, it doesn't, Father. A lot of people get drunk and God doesn't blast them with lightning."

"God blasted you with lightning?"

"Yes, and blew everything to hell. The whole pier. I fell in and almost drowned..."

"Wait, wait. Slow down, my son. You're losing me. Let me get this straight. You were drunk on a pier throwing puppets in the ocean..."

"And a crucifix."

"Yes, and a crucifix and you got hit by lightning?"

"The whole pier got hit."

"That may not have been God. It might have just been the weather."

"It wasn't the weather. Does the weather have a big hand in it? When I was drowning I looked up and I saw God's Hand."

"When you were under water?"

"Where else would I be drowning? I'm sorry, Father. I know this sounds crazy. I'm just scared."

"There's nothing to be afraid of."

"That is easy for you to say. God didn't do anything to you."

"Did He do something to you besides blast you with lightning?"

"Oh yes."

"Like what?"

"Well, when I saw the Hand in the ocean, I grabbed it. That's all I remember till I woke up on the beach."

"So He saved you from drowning. That's a good thing."

"I am not so sure. When I woke up I felt really terrible."

"That makes sense. You'd been struck by lightning. Did you go to a hospital?"

"Yes." Jorge groaned and buried his face in his hands. "Father, do you believe in demons?"

"Why do you ask?"

"When I was driving to the hospital, I saw demons flying in the air. They were black and they had huge wings. They're all over Los Angeles."

"Why does that not surprise me?"

"When I got to the hospital, there was a big demon in a room and I think I killed it."

"How did you manage that?"

"I touched it with my hand, the one God grabbed. And here is the weird part.

"We haven't gotten to the weird part yet?"

"After I killed the demon, I healed a little blind girl. I touched her eyes with my hand and she can see, Father. She was blind as a rock. I'm sorry about the crucifix. It was a stupid thing to do. One other thing, it came back into my truck out of the ocean all by itself and now I'm afraid to touch it."

"The puppets didn't come back?"

"Father, forget about the puppets."

"They're hard to forget about. All right. Well, I think I've got a good picture of everything."

"But I'm not finished yet. I haven't told you the scariest part. After I healed the little girl...I went blind myself."

"I see. But you're not blind right now."

"It went away during the night. While I was at the hospital, I crashed into a bunch of boxes and they knocked me out. When I woke up, I could see again."

"My son, I have only one more question."

"What is it, father?"

"How much did you have to drink this morning?"

"Nothing. Not a drop. I swear. Well, I don't swear. I promise. Not today. What I need is something to make God leave me alone. Just give me some penance, Father, something really awful. That's what I need."

"I'm going to give you a business card, my son."

"A business card?"

He slid a card under the screen. "It's for a psychiatrist. I want you to go see him and the church will pay for it."

"You think I'm loco?"

"I think you're...a little disturbed."

"But hasn't this happened to people before? Aren't there books about people who heal other people?"

"I don't know of any."

"What about the Bible?"

"Well, there is that."

"It could happen again, Father, I can feel it. And I've got to stop it before it does. I mean, what if I went blind while I was driving. So I heal a little girl and kill fifty people on a sidewalk. You see what I mean?"

"I do. Yes, I do. My son, you need some peace and quiet."

"No, I need some penance."

"All right, penance. I want you to say ten 'Hail, Marys' each day for a week."

"That's it? Seventy 'Hail Marys'?"

"That, and go to the psychiatrist."

"But, that's not nearly enough, Father. I get that much for telling a lie."

"Have you ever been to a psychiatrist, my son?"

"No."

"Trust me, it's enough. Now, go in peace, your sins are forgiven."

Jorge stared at the screen in total frustration.

Half an hour later, his truck slid into a parking space at the Los Angeles Public Library. Jumping out, he ran up the steps. Inside, he hurried to the main desk. An austere librarian stared suspiciously at his clothes.

"May I help you, sir?"

"I need some books."

"About what?"

"Healing people. You know...touching them and making them well?"

"Touching people and making them well?"

"I don't mean like, 'how-to-do-it'. Just... books about it. By doctors. You know...to read?"

"I suggest that you go to the computer and see what you can find under the H's."

Jorge's mouth went dry. "The...computer?"

"Yes, over there?" She pointed to a long computer station in the center of the room that was surrounded by grade school children.

Completely intimidated, Jorge headed toward it. Then he stood in front of one of the terminals not knowing what to do and feeling like an idiot. The children were deep at work and they weren't having any trouble at all. Carefully, he touched a key. A boy of ten with thick glasses was watching him.

"You don't have to be afraid of it. It won't explode. What are you looking for?" He moved to Jorge's terminal.

"I am looking for books about healing."

The kid typed in the word. Instantly, the screen filled with data. The boy looked up at Jorge. "Your category's too broad. Be more specific. Homeopathic medicine? Psychological factors in healing? Quantitative research methodology and the healing process. The list goes on for pages."

Miserably, Jorge replied, "Is there something about...touching people and making them well?"

The boy stared up at him as though he had just arrived from another planet. "Maybe we should start with comic books."

CHAPTER ELEVEN

Christmas in Wonderland

Eddie Gartman wandered between cars in the crowded parking lot of a shopping mall. His book was under his arm and he was wearing the blanket wrapped around his head like a sloppy, flapping turban. Masses of people were heading toward an entrance under a sign that read, "Christmas Wonderland Sale – Visit Santa."

As he came close to the doors, Eddie heard bells and choir music. He froze. "Mr. Bunley-Mr.Bunley, singing place!!" Overjoyed, he pushed through the people into the building.

Once inside, he found himself in a perfume department. Eddie stared at the women clustered at the counters. Rushing up to one of them who was looking at herself in a mirror, he yelled, "Lips,

lips. Biiiig." Then he pursed his lips and blew through them, spitting all over her. Laughing uproariously, he hurried on through the store.

As Eddie dodged people in the aisles, his blanket snagged several delicately stacked displays, pulling them down into crashing heaps. He didn't notice. All he cared about was that the choir music and bells were getting louder.

He began singing tunelessly at the top of his voice, "La-la-la-la-la-la-la-la..."

Leaving the store, he entered the central mall. Instantly, he was in heaven. Cascading down from the ceiling three stories above were thousands and thousands of white lights that seemed to swirl in a blizzard that stretched as far as he could see. Dangling in the lights were hundreds of large, mirrored snowflakes, that flashed in a rainbow of colors.

Beneath this avalanche and running the length of the mall was a forest of ten-foot-tall, white Christmas trees loaded with glistening ornaments. Suspended high between them were life-size reindeer that seemed to be prancing in mid-air.

With wide eyes, Eddie wandered through this stupendously cheesy tableau, so excited that he could hardly breathe.

At the center of it all rose a mountain that looked like something out of diabetes hell. Spilling down it was a lava flow of candy – monstrous, silver-wrapped kisses, chocolate soldiers large enough to go to war, six-foot peppermint canes, marshmallow stars the size of truck tires and sugar pinwheels that could have powered small towns and all were suspended in a fiery river of glitzy cellophane.

Perched at the top in a swathe of faux fur and twinkling lights, was a red and white throne half-buried in fake cotton candy. On it lounged a jolly Santa with a belly that matched the mountain. Periodically, he would belch out a "HO, HO, HO," which didn't sound quite convincing.

Snaking through the store up to Santa's mountain was a long line of children and parents waiting to share their Christmas wishes and get pictures taken.

Lines meant nothing to Eddie. When he saw the mountain with Santa at the top, he crowed with ecstasy and started running. Pushing through the crowd, he stumbled and lurched up the steps to the throne.

A little girl was just sliding off Santa's ample lap. Eddie took the opportunity to plop down hard. He was much larger than any child and the jolly old elf groaned under his weight.

"Uhhhh…aren't you a little big for this?"

Eddie giggled. Santa shifted around so he could look at his face. Instantly, he understood, but that didn't help the fact that he was being squashed.

"Do we…have a parent…with this young man?"

No one answered from the crowd. A gorgeous Santa's Helper moved up beside him.

"Santa, he didn't sign up for a picture and I'm afraid he cut in line."

Santa grunted, "Would you…move just a little bit, son? You're crushing Santa's privates."

The old man managed to shift Eddie, who stared at him as though he were an angel.

"Just a little more. Okay, good. That's better. So… what's your name?"

Eddie stuck his face two inches from the bewhiskered nose and laughed uproariously.

"Christmas-Christmas. Fat-fat-fat. Beeeer." He reached down, grabbed Santa's belly and shook it."

"Hey, hey. Don't do that. It hurts."

"Beeeer! Faaaat," Eddie croaked.

"Yeah, right, beer, fat. Grab me like that again and I'm gonna throw your butt outta here." Quickly, Santa slid back into character. "Santa doesn't like to have his guts shaken, especially right after he's eaten a sausage pizza."

Eddie laughed in his face again.

"All right, what do you want for Christmas?"

There was no answer. Eddie just stared at him.

"You want a train or a bicycle? How about membership in a weight loss program?"

Still, there was no answer.

"Look, Santa wants to bring you something for Christmas, but unless you get off my legs, I'm gonna be doing it in a wheelchair. Okay, your turn's over. Get off me."

He started to move Eddie off his lap, but Eddie threw his arms around his neck with a grip so tight it choked him.

"No-no-no-no-no-no. Can't go. Can't go. Mr. Bunley."

Santa croaked, "Hep. I need hep."

Two of his lovely assistants came to the rescue. They tried to pull Eddie off, but he was far too strong.

One of them snarled, "Come on, now. Santa's got other children to talk to. Don't make us call the cops."

Still, Eddie hung on, "No-no-no-no-no-no..."

Santa was turning blue. His eyes were beginning to bulge out.

One of the helpers grabbed a fistful of candy canes. "Here. Look here. Look, what I've got for you."

Eddie stared, then broke his choke-hold and reached for them.

Quickly, the helper stepped back from the throne and Eddie followed her.

Released from his bondage, Santa gasped for air. "That's it. I'm finished. I can't take this crap anymore. Kids peeing on me, little brats puking in my beard, sneezing their snot in my mouth. And now I get choked by a retard. I was safer in Folsom."

Struggling off his throne, he started down the mountain. The next child in line began howling, "Santa, Santa, don't go."

The kid's father yelled, "Hey, we've been waiting for an hour. Get back up there. You can't leave."

"Watch me, jackass."

"Jackass? You call me a jackass? I'm gonna kick your ass."

Santa rushed away, with the father after him. All the kids in the line started howling. Several fathers joined the chase.

Eddie was oblivious to all of it. Sucking a fistful of candy canes, his face and hands covered with goo, he continued his journey through Christmas Wonderland.

As he meandered between the flocked trees, the singing and bells grew louder. When he reached the far end of the mall, Eddie stepped out of the forest. In front of him, a crowd was gathered listening to a choir. The singers were dressed in Edwardian costumes and stood on risers. Around them rose stacks of gigantic, fake Christmas presents. On the boxes, in blinking lights, were the names of all the stores in the mall. Above the presents, grinning elf faces the size of elephant heads leered down at the crowd, as though, at any moment, they might devour them.

The choir was singing, "Jingle Bells." The first row of musicians were playing hand bells that were set out on a long table.

Pushing to the front, Eddie stared. He watched with delight as the shiny bells were lifted and rung. He whispered, "Mr. Bunley-Mr.Bunley-bells-bells-bells-bells..."

Moving very close to the table, he squatted down so that his nose was inches from the shiny metal. This was a little disconcerting to the players.

Laughing, Eddie called out, "Bells. Bong-bong-bong-bong-bong-bong..."

For a moment, he was content to watch. But then a choir member set down a huge bell right in front of him and the temptation was just too great. Eddie picked it up.

The bell player hissed, "Hey, put that down."

But, Eddie didn't put it down. Instead, he picked up another one.

"Bells. Bong-bong-bong-bong-bong..." He started ringing them as hard as he could.

Quickly, the singing turned to chaos. The bell player yelled, "Gimme the damn bells."

The man grabbed for them. This instigated a serious tug of war across the table.

"My bells. My bells. Mr. Bunley-help-help-help-help-bong-bong-bong-bong-bong..."

Finally, Eddie jerked the bells free, knocking over the whole table. Then, he ran straight up the risers through the choir. The singers went flying.

Several yelled, "Get him!"

They tried to grab him, but he got away. A security guard saw the chaos and the chase was on.

Ringing the bells with all his might, Eddie jumped from the top riser into the huge wrapped boxes. As he climbed through them, the giant elf faces came unhinged and crashed down. When he reached the top, there was nowhere to go and everyone was after him, so he jumped onto one of the white Christmas trees. This fell beneath his weight, taking out reindeer and snowflakes that broke from their moorings.

The chain reaction was horrific. As Eddie crashed on and on, knocking down trees, everything in the mall started falling. Suddenly, the lights didn't just look like a cascade, they were a three story cascade of popping, flashing electricity. It was Christmas in hell with shoppers screaming and running.

As he ran through the destruction, Eddie lost his bells. But in the chaos, he managed to disappear in the crowd.

Fire trucks, police and ambulances shrieked to the mall entrance. From outside in the parking lot, Eddie watched stoically.

"Not the Singing Place. Not-not-not-not." Shaking his head, he walked away.

The large room of the I.N.S. Building was as busy as ever. All the cubicles were filled with people trying to deal with immigration problems. Into the room walked Dr. Finnegan. With him was a very stern-faced man in a three-piece suit, carrying a briefcase.

Finnegan stopped at a desk and asked a question. The young woman behind the desk pointed down the row to Mr. Stoner, who was busily at work on his computer. The two men strode over to him.

"Mr. Stoner?"

"Yes?"

"My name is Dr. William Finnegan. This is my attorney, Mr. Arnold Brill. I believe you're handling the case of Jorge Mendoza and his family."

"I'm sorry, all of our cases are confidential."

Finnegan towered over him, smiling in his most deadly manner. "Yes, I understand that. Mr. Stoner, before we begin our conversation, I should make you aware that my brother is Mr. Arthur Finnegan, Under Secretary of State for Central American Affairs in Washington, D.C. A faxed letter of instructions from his office is about to be received by the director of your department. It has to do with Mr. Mendoza, Mrs. Mendoza and their daughter. As I prepare to insert that letter up your rectal region, may I suggest that you bring up their file on your screen?"

Staring at him wide-eyed, Stoner turned to the computer.

CHAPTER TWELVE

Monsterworld

It was night and Jorge Mendoza lay sprawled on his bed. Spread around him were books with titles such as "Healing Delusions and the Modern Mind" and "Psychological Metaphors and Healing Strategies." He was struggling through a turgid volume entitled: "Case Studies in Psychosomatic Healing: A Report of the Medical Association of America." Finally, he threw it down.

"*Nothing!* They don't tell me nothing. And they don't tell me nothing, because they don't know nothing."

Getting up, he walked over to the work table. Lying on it was an open Bible.

"And this! I read this, but it makes me crazy. 'He took up our sicknesses and carried our sorrows. By his wounds we are healed.' That's about God. I am not God."

He stared at the ceiling. "Please, I am very glad that Ginny got healed, but I don't want to do this no more. Give it to somebody else."

He buried his face in his hands. "The Father is right. I am loco. And why am I loco? I talk to puppets for so many years. Do grown men talk to puppets? They do not. Only me. And the puppets talk back. Ha, ha, very much fun until you go nuts. Now, maybe nothing is real. Ginny didn't get healed. I am in a nut-house and everything is just in my head."

Feeling miserable, he walked into the bathroom. After dousing his face with water, Jorge stared into the mirror. He was exhausted. His eyes were bloodshot and the wrinkles around them seemed deeper.

"I am so tired. I need to sleep."

He was about to leave the room, when he heard a whisper.

Then another.

"No. No, no, no, no." He covered his ears. "Go away! Leave me alone!"

The whispers grew louder until they were all around him. Then, came the crackling sound like fire in dry grass. He looked down at his hand.

On it appeared the rippling light and the drop of crimson.

"Stop it!"

He drenched his hand with water. Then he scrubbed it hard with soap. But the light wouldn't go away, it only grew brighter.

"Please God, do not do this to me again."

Rushing to his bed, Jorge covered his head with a blanket. But the whispers wouldn't stop. And with them was a new sound. It was the flapping of mighty wings as though something were flying toward him. Suddenly, he felt wind.

Pulling away the blanket, Jorge looked up...and *yelled*.

Staring down at him from the ceiling was one of the terrifying angel vultures. Its flapping wings filled the top of the room. But this one wasn't black; it was burning red as though it had come straight from the fires of hell. Long arms with talons were reaching for him.

With a shriek, Jorge jumped up and ran into the hall. Then he rushed outside to his truck and drove away.

Eddie Gartman was walking down a dark street, arguing with the ever unseen Mr. Bunley.

"No-no-no-no-no-no-no. Going-home-going-home-going-home. Where-where? One-

one-two-six,   one-one-two-six.   Shut-up-Mr.Bunley.   Shut-up-shut-up-one-one-two six, one-one-two-six, somewhere-somewhere."

Covering his ears, he yelled the numbers. *"One-one-two-six, one one-two-six, not-listening-not-listening- one-one-two-six, one- one-two-six...where?"*

He turned a corner. Down the street, he saw bright lights and heard music. For a moment, he stood as though not knowing what to do. Then he looked at the cover of his book, The Singing Place.

Very tired, he whispered, "Okay. Okay-okay-okay-okay-okay."

Slowly, Eddie shuffled toward the garish lights and sounds.

Jorge Mendoza raced through the city going nowhere as fast as he could. He was sweating and trembling. His hand glistened on the steering wheel. Trickles of blood ran from his palm, the drops vanishing into thin air. As he stared at the crucifix dangling from the mirror, the whispers echoed around him. But at least there wasn't any of the horrible fog. And there weren't any monsters flapping around the buildings.

He turned a corner...and screeched to a stop.

A block ahead, fifty feet in the air, hovered the beautiful and mysterious Pillar of Light. To escape it, he veered down a side street. But it was there too. He turned another corner. There it was again.

And then came the unearthly singing.

On this street, he was in a crowd. Hundreds of people were moving in one direction and they were all around him.

At that moment, Jorge's engine died. He tried to start it, but it wouldn't even turn over. Everything electrical in the truck had shut down. His headlights, his display, all of it had gone dark. He turned the key again. Nothing. Pounding the steering wheel, he yelled in frustration.

Finally, there was nothing to do but get out. The people were heading toward the entrance to a tacky carnival. A shiny red and green banner invited everyone to enter...

CHRISTMAS STARLAND.

As Jorge stared at it, the singing, that only he could hear, grew louder. And everything around him began to change.

The whole world grew black. The buildings were so dark that he could barely see their outlines. He couldn't even see the street beneath his shoes. The only light was the dazzling neon of the carnival, which shimmered in the blackness with a surreal glow. The people heading toward it were a blurred crowd of ghosts glistening in the night.

There was a crimson flash.

Jorge looked up. Directly above him blazed the Pillar of Light. Slowly, it began to descend.

Jorge ran.

And the only direction to run was where the crowd was going. Craning his neck to see the sky, he rushed toward the carnival entrance. Then, like a hunted dog, he pushed and stumbled down the midway – past the twisting rides and games of chance, the food booths and brassy sideshows. A mass of ghost people were streaming into a tent where a barker was yelling,

SEE THE
MERRY CHRISTMAS FREAKS
STUPENDOUS!
STARTLING!
AMAZING!
TALK TO THE
TWO-HEADED SANTA!
FEED RUDOLPH
THE REINDEER BOY!
LAUGH AT ELLIE
THE 700 POUND ELF!
COME ONE, COME ALL TO

CHRISTMAS IN JOLLY STARLAND
(Parental Discretion Advised)

The crowd was full of children. But to Jorge they were like shadows and, as he ran past, no one saw him at all. Finally, exhausted, he had to stop. Bent over, gasping for air, he looked up.

He was in front of a fun house called Monsterworld. Bizarre Christmas carols, twisted almost beyond recognition, blared from loudspeakers. No one was going in. It seemed deserted. Above the entrance hung the Pillar of Light.

"So...here you are. Wherever I run...you are there. And I am too tired...to run anymore. You bring me...to Monsterworld? Is that where I belong?"

As though in answer, the Light drifted down. For a moment, it hung in front of the entrance, then it disappeared inside.

"You want me to go in there, but you don't tell me why. I don't want to go in there. Does that matter to you? It does not. If I don't go in, what will you do? I know what you will do. I am like a rabbit and you are like a hound. You will chase me forever and I cannot escape. I think even if I go to hell, you will be waiting."

Slowly, Jorge stood up. From inside the tent came a strange, golden glow.

"All right, all right, maybe this time you will kill me and I will be done with it."

Shaking his head, he dragged himself toward the entrance.

Once inside, to his disgust, Jorge discovered that he was in a maze of rooms filled with steam and leering monster faces all decorated in a happy holiday motif. With the pounding music and screeching recorded laughter, it was like Christmas in a torture chamber.

"So here I am. Jorge with the monsters. But I do not see anything. What am I supposed to do?"

He waited and nothing happened.

"Maybe you want me to wander. How do I know? How do I know anything? So I will wander."

Covering his ears, he passed through one door after another. And each room was weirder than the last. When he reached the room of the Christmas Zombies, it was all he could take. Snarling with disgust, he pushed through a door...and stopped.

Eddie Gartman stood alone in a room full of wonderful strangeness. All around him were mirrors that distorted his body. Each was embedded in the mouth of a monster face dangling with cheesy Christmas lights. Thousands of fake stars blinked on the ceiling and thick steam swirled up to his knees.

But Eddie didn't see the ugliness. He was enraptured. With his arms raised, holding the book in one hand and the blanket in the other, he spun in circles croaking, "Music-music-la-la-la-la-la music-la-la-la-la-la-la-la..."

Then, catching his reflection in a mirror, he stopped. The image was grotesque. Stepping toward it, he laughed.

"Mr. Bunley, Mr. Bunley, funny, funny."

He moved to the next one. It was even more horrible. This time, he didn't laugh. On he went, from mirror to mirror, seeing one distorted image of himself after another. Finally, at the end, hung a single undistorted mirror.

Eddie stood in front of it and touched his reflection. Tears were in his eyes, as he whispered, "Ugly. Ugly."

At the opposite end of the room stood Jorge Mendoza. Tears were in his eyes too, but they were tears of rage. Slowly, he walked forward toward the nightmare that only he could see.

Hanging above Eddie, with its black wings outstretched was one of the angel vultures. Both of its long arms were reaching down and its talons were buried deep in Eddie's back.

Jorge looked down at his hand. It was covered with rippling light. When he reached Eddie Gartman, he stopped.

The black-winged creature was above him. Through its talons, it was sucking life. The thing turned its head and stared at him with huge black eyes. Then it looked down at his hand and into those eyes came terror.

Jorge heard a shriek of rage. But the sound didn't come through his ears, it came straight into his mind. After the shriek, in his head he heard a screeching voice that sounded like a buzz saw cutting steel spewing the most horrifying curses that he had ever heard against God, against Jesus and against him. Over and over it rasped, "We will kill you, we will rip you, we will slash you..."

In his mind, Jorge spoke to it. "I am not afraid of you. I see what you do to people. This poor man's pain is not enough. You take what little life he has and fill him with sorrow. You tear his heart."

Jorge stepped closer. "But you cannot do these things forever. God will not allow it. Do you know where this blood comes from? I think it comes from Jesus, the Great King, who died on the cross. And do you know why He died? Yes, I think you do."

As he spoke, the thing tried to pull its talons out of Eddie to escape, but it couldn't.

Jorge smiled, "What, you cannot get away? I wonder why?"

He drew closer. It screeched and writhed.

Jorge lifted his hand, "This is the Blood of Heaven. I have run from it, but I will not run anymore."

Reaching up with his other hand, Jorge grabbed the vulture's body and pulled. Dead, rotting flesh tore away. Then, Jorge lifted his blood-filled hand and stuck it straight into the hole. There was a scream that echoed from the depths of hell. The talons pulled out of Eddie Gartman.

Jorge wouldn't withdraw his hand and the thing couldn't escape him. As it shrieked and thrashed, Living Fire spread into its bones, through its flesh, to its skin and wings. Finally, with a last croak of rage, one of it talons slashed Jorge's face from forehead to chin, tearing it open to the bone.

He staggered and almost fell.

The fire roared and the monster was gone.

With his bloody hand, Jorge reached out and touched the back of Eddie Gartman's head. Eddie gasped and turned. Their eyes met.

Staring at Jorge, Eddie fell against the mirror. "Who...Who...Who...Who...?"

But Jorge couldn't speak. His face was ripped and flesh was hanging down, but there was no blood.

Eddie yelled, *"Who-who-who-who-who?"* Then, he turned and ran.

Jorge stumbled to the mirror. Leaning against it, he stared in shock. The thing had slashed him to the bone. He could see his skull. But, as he watched, the flesh around the wound pulled together, healing into a terrible, jagged scar.

CHAPTER THIRTEEN

Finding Home

Jorge stood alone in the room of mirrors with the crashing music of Monsterworld clanging in his ears. He was surrounded by the distorted images of himself. Above him dangled the universe of fake stars.

But slowly, the clanging music began to fade. In its place Jorge heard strange melodies that rose and swirled and faded and above him every star refracted into a rainbow. The ceiling was covered with millions of tiny rainbows. He was standing in another world, a world as seen through Eddie Gartman's eyes.

Suddenly, he heard a creaky, sing-song voice. "Eddie, Eddie, come on and get ready, it's time to find the fun. Eddie, Eddie, come on and get ready, it's time to run and run."

Jorge looked around. In a mirror, appeared the vague image of a strange little man barely two feet tall and dressed in bright rags.

He was dancing a jig and singing, "There'll be a smile on every face. I'll pull a rabbit from a vase...(he did it), but we have to find The Singing Place, The Singing Place, The Singing Place..."

Over and over, the singsong repeated. Jorge rubbed his eyes. Once more, he stared into the mirror. His face didn't look quite right and it wasn't just the scar. Small changes had begun. He heard laughter.

The weird little man was in the mirror too. "We have to find The Singing Place, The Singing Place, The Singing Place."

Jorge ran from the room.

Bursting out of the fun house, he stumbled down the steps. As he ran down the midway, one of his legs didn't work exactly right. His running was uneven, but Jorge barely noticed. He had entered another reality. Through Eddie's eyes, the carnival was a swirling blizzard of sights and sounds. Rides flashed with fire. The neon was a rainbow blur. Music jangled and roared. It was all so gorgeously insane that Jorge laughed wildly.

"Look at this. Look at this. Look-look-look-look."

No longer did the people look like ghosts. While he croaked with laughter, they stared at him. Realizing it, he hurried away. But as Jorge moved deeper and deeper into Eddie's surreal world, new images appeared. In front of him was a carousel. Suddenly, memories came that were not his own.

He was Eddie riding on a carousel. On the horse next to him was the weird little man. And now he knew his name.

Mr. Bunley.

It was Mr. Bunley.

The ugly face was laughing at him. And as he laughed, the carousel went faster and faster. The memory dissolved in a swirl of fiery light.

When it was gone, Jorge was dizzy. "Oh, my God..."

He started walking. But a few steps farther he passed several tough-looking teenage boys playing a carnival game. Instantly, there was another memory.

Eddie Gartman was surrounded by the gang. He yelled as they rushed him, picking him up and throwing him into the dumpster.

And Jorge yelled.

It was like falling into an abyss. When those images were gone, he was terrified. "I am in hell."

Staring at the teenagers, he turned and ran.

Jorge rushed out of the carnival and ran down the street to where he had left his truck. It was still there. He jumped in. This time, when he turned the key, the engine started without any problem. He was about to drive away, when he heard the singsong voice.

"Eddie, Eddie, come on and get ready. It's time to find the fun. Eddie, Eddie, come on and get ready, we'll run and run and run."

Jorge spun around. In the dark glass of a store window, he saw the huge reflection of Mr. Bunley.

He yelled, *"I am not-not Eddie. Leave me alone."*

The face vanished.

Instantly, another vivid memory began. Eddie Gartman was sitting on a couch in his living room. Beside him was his mother. From her came a warm, wonderful glow. Though old, she was still beautiful and she was reading the Mr. Bunley book to him.

"Eddie, Eddie, aren't we glad we got ready. We've run and run and run. Eddie, Eddie, aren't we glad we got ready. We've had so very much fun."

She closed the book.

Jorge heard Eddie's voice coming from his own lips, "Mommy-Mommy-Mommy-read-it-read-it-read-it again. Please-please-please-please..."

But as he spoke, the smiling mother slowly vanished away.

"No. Don't-don't. Don't-don't-don't. Come back. *Come back*." He couldn't help it, tears began streaming down his cheeks.

"Gone. Gone-gone."

Struggling to breathe through deep sobs, Jorge put the truck into gear and drove off into the darkness.

An exhausted and terrified Eddie Gartman ran down a street several blocks from the carnival. Leaning against a building, he held his head.

"Mommy. Mommy-mommy. My head. Hurts-hurts....it hurts."

Subtle changes had begun. His face wasn't quite as misshapen as before and his body was slimmer. But the changes were causing pain. He saw an old phone booth across the street.

"Call. Call, call, call, mommy."

As he ran toward it, several cars almost hit him. Horns blared, but he didn't notice.

"Got to, got to, got to."

But when he got inside the booth, there was no phone. With tears of frustration, he began pounding on the glass. *"Got-to-call-her-got-to-call-her-got -to-call-her-got-to-call-her..."* Finally, he slumped to the floor and sobbed.

A late model Mercedes pulled up and parked outside Jorge Mendoza's apartment building. Dr. Finnegan got out. After looking at an address on a small card, he climbed the stairs to the entrance.

Finnegan made his way down a hall, checking apartment numbers. Finally, he came to Jorge's door. He was about to knock, when he heard a voice inside yelling, *"No. Get-get away. Leave me alone. You're not...you're not-not real. Stop-stop that singing."*

Deeply concerned, Finnegan knocked.

From inside, Jorge's voice answered, "Who-who's there?"

"Jorge, it's Bill Finnegan from the hospital. I was worried about you this morning. I thought I'd drop by and see how you were doing."

"I'm-I'm fine. Please. Please-please. Go. Away."

"Jorge..."

"I said-said, go away."

Finnegan stared at the door. The voice coming from inside sounded very odd. His worry deepened. Turning, he walked down the hall. Minutes later, he knocked on the door of the building manager. A woman answered.

"Yes?"

"Good evening. I'm Dr. William Finnegan from Children's Hospital." He handed a business card to her. "I'm sorry to bother you, but a person is ill in apartment 312 and can't open the door. Would you open it for me?"

"Sure. Let me get the key."

Finnegan and the manager hurried up to Jorge's door. The woman inserted the key and opened it.

"If you need anything else, doctor..."

"Thank you. I'll let you know."

As she walked away, Jorge came out of the bathroom. When he saw the open door, he rushed to a corner.

"No. No-no."

With his back turned, he stood hugging himself. Finnegan entered and shut the door.

"I'm sorry to go to the manager, Jorge, but something's wrong and I want to help you."

"Can't...can't-can't...do... nothing."

"I'm sure I can, if you'll let me. What's going on here? Turn around and let me look at you."

Slowly, Jorge turned. The beginning of Eddie's soft deformities were distorting his face and from forehead to chin was the terrible scar.

Finnegan was so horrified, he could barely speak, "My God…"

Suddenly, Mr. Bunley's song grew very loud and insistent in Jorge's ears.

"…I'll put a smile on every face, but we've got to find the singing place, the singing place, the singing place."

"Shut-shut up."

"What?"

With a snarl of rage, Jorge rushed into the bathroom and up to the mirror.

The ugly little man was staring back at him. Jorge smashed the glass, but the face remained in the fragments and the echoing song continued.

"Leave-leave me alone. I am not-not-not Eddie."

Totally shaken, Finnegan pulled Jorge from the mirror.

"What has happened to you? Let me look at your face? My God, that scar…" He touched it. "Come on, we've got to get you to the hospital."

Jorge backed away. "No! No-no-no-no-no-no…Won't-do, won't do… any, any… good." Then, he held his head in his hands and groaned.

"Jorge, what has happened to you?"

A flashing memory.

Suddenly, Jorge was in Eddie's living room. There were crashing sounds and terrifying, skewed images. He saw people carrying furniture out of the house. They moved as though in a roaring rush. Jorge pushed past Finnegan into the other room.

"Stop. Stop-stop-stop-stop-stop..."

The memory ended.

"Oh God. Sad-Sad. So. Sad. Scared."

Finnegan pulled out his cell phone, "I'm calling an ambulance."

Jorge grabbed his hand. "No. Listen-listen. Please..." Desperately, he struggled for words. "Hospital. In-in the hospital...the little girl. Name. Name-name. What...is...it? Ginny. Ginny-Ginny. Remember?"

Finnegan stared at him.

"Blind? Can't-can't see?"

"You mean Ginny Conlon?"

"Yes. Yes. Yes. Her. I...I... touched." He pointed to his eyes. "I touched...touched."

"What?"

"I...*touched.*" He touched his own eyes. *"Me. I...did it.* In. In-the room. Her room. Hers. I...did it. Then...went blind. My...self. Blind. Ginny...sees."

"What are you saying?"

Jorge grabbed one of the books on healing and pounded his finger on the cover, *"Touched. Touched-touched-touched-touched..."*

Finnegan stared at the book, then back at him.

"You're telling me that you're the one who healed Ginny Conlon?"

Jorge nodded his head over and over. "Yes. Yes. Yes. Then...blind. Me. Her on my-my eyes. Later. After-after...see again."

"I don't understand."

"Her-her blind...then, me, me, me."

"You're saying...that when she was healed...you became blind?"

"Yes-yes-yes-yes. *Now-again-now. New this one. The same."*

"This is insanity. Jorge, I don't know what's happened to you, but, you're very ill. If you don't come with me right now, I'm calling for help."

Jorge closed his eyes, "Oh God...Jesus-Jesus help me."

Jorge held his head and sat down in a chair.

Another flashing image began.

He was in Eddie's empty bedroom...humming four notes over and over. Rocking in the chair.

Julie's face bent close. Her voice echoed. "Eddie, if you don't come right now, I'm going to get Alex and Steve from next door and they're going to carry you out."

The memory ended. Julie's face was replaced by that of Dr. Finnegan.

"Jorge..."

Tears were in Jorge's eyes. "Okay. Okay-okay-okay-okay..." He looked up at the doctor. "See-things...things-things...they-see."

The doctor pulled him to his feet, "Come on, let's go." He tried to lead him from the room, but Jorge pulled back.

"NO. No-no. Help...me. Help me...find-find him."

"What?"

"Find. Him. One I-I-I...touched. Now Lost. Lost-lost. Please."

Dr. Finnegan stared at him. "You...touched someone else? That's why you think you're like this?"

Jorge nodded vehemently. "Like Ginny-Ginny. Help me...while...I...can still..think.

"Who was this person?"

Jorge closed his eyes in desperate concentration.

"Name. Eddie. Eddie...something something."

"You don't know his name?"

"Eddie...Gart...man. Gart...man"

"Where is he?"

"Looking-for...Looking-for...the-Singing-Place. Can't-find. Looking. Looking. Looking. Looking."

"Where does this Eddie Gart...man live?"

There was a flashing image. Suddenly, before his eyes appeared the front of Eddie's house.

"Live...lives-lives...one-one-two six, one-one-two-six...someplace-someplace..."

Mr. Bunley's song began again. "Eddie, Eddie, come on and get ready, it's time to find the fun. Eddie, Eddie come on and get ready, we'll run and run and run..."

"Shut-up-shut-up-Mr.Bunley. One one two six, one one two six...France... France...Franciosa."

With sweat dripping in his eyes, Jorge stared at Dr. Finnegan. "Find him.....Please. Please-please."

Finnegan shook his head, "I don't believe any of this." Bending close, he examined the scar. "Since I saw you this morning your face has been viciously slashed...and completely healed. That is impossible. *How did that happen?*"

Jorge stared at him and said, "Find-find...him... please."

A strange look came into Finnegan's eyes. "Your face is changing more."

"No time-time. Please..."

"All right, we'll go look for this person as long as you promise to go to the hospital afterward."

Jorge nodded.

CHAPTER FOURTEEN

The Singing Place

D r. Finnegan's Mercedes drove slowly down Eddie Gartman's street. Finnegan looked at the house numbers. "Okay, that's it over there, 1126 Franciosa." A light was on in the living room.

Jorge stared at the house and smiled. The transformation of his face and body were almost complete.

"Yes. Yes-yes-yes-yes-yes..."

Finnegan pulled the car into the driveway and stopped. Jumping out, Jorge ran to the front door and tried to open it. But it was locked. The doctor came and rang the bell.

An exhausted Julie Gartman appeared, "Yes?

Jorge was overjoyed. "Julie. Julie-Julie-Julie-Julie..."

"Do I know you?"

"Julie-Julie-Julie."

Finnegan said, "We're sorry to bother you, ma'am. We're looking for someone named Eddie Gart...man."

"That's my brother. But he's not here. He ran away yesterday and we can't find him."

"Does your brother have Down Syndrome?"

"Yes."

"And your name is Julie?

"Julie Gartman."

"I'm Dr. Finnegan from Children's Hospital. This is Jorge Mendoza. Have you ever seen him before?"

"No, but maybe he knows my brother. Eddie went to a workshop for a while."

"Ms. Gartman, do you mind if we come in?"

Before she could fully open the door, Jorge pushed past into the living room.

"I'm sorry I can't ask you to sit down. My mother died and I've sold everything."

Jorge stared around. Suddenly, he was seeing the room as Eddie remembered it--filled with furniture. He began walking around, touching things that no one else could see. Tears came to his eyes.

"Home. Home. Home. Home."

In a rocking chair, he saw Eddie's mother. The warm glow was all around her.

"Mommy. Mommy, my turn. My turn. Back-and-forth-back-and-forth-back-and-forth..."

Julie stared at him. It was the eeriest thing she'd ever seen. "That's where my mother used to sit. That's what my brother used to say to her."

Jorge entered the bedroom. The rocking chair was still there. Sitting on it, he began to rock and hum the same four notes that Eddie had hummed...over and over.

Julie was freaked. "What is going on here?"

Dr. Finnegan shook his head, "I'm not sure, Ms. Gartman, but I think it's very important for us to find your brother."

"The police have been searching since yesterday morning. I drove around all last night myself. No one can find him."

"Was his picture on television?"

She nodded.

"I saw it. Do you mind if we look for him together?"

"No, but what good will it do?"

"Jorge may be able to help us."

Julie, Dr. Finnegan and Jorge left the house and walked toward Dr. Finnegan's car. Suddenly, Jorge stopped and stared at Julie's mini-van.

"No. No-no-no-no. In-in there. Going-going away." Walking over he touched the car window.

"Inside. Riding-riding-riding. Eddie scared. Scared-scared."

Finnegan looked questioningly at Julie.

"I was taking my brother to live in a group home when he got out of the car and ran off. But how does he know that?"

"Maybe we should retrace the route you took. Do you mind if we use your car?"

"I don't understand."

"Neither do I, but I think we have to try this."

Julie opened the car door, but Jorge didn't want to get in.

"No. Don't-don't-don't. Scared... scared."

"Oh, God..." Julie was trembling.

Finnegan grasped Jorge's shoulders. "Jorge, listen to me. You are not Eddie Gartman. We are *looking* for Eddie. You've got to help us find him. Do you understand?"

Jorge stared at him. Finally, they got him into the car. Very shaken, Julie slid in behind the wheel.

Hugging his book and blanket, Eddie Gartman rushed down a city street. His face was continuing an incredible change. It still bore some of the marks of the past, but they were almost gone.

"Mr. Bunley, Mr. Bunley, where are you? I hear you, but I can't see you anymore."

Suddenly, he heard music and stopped. It was the carillon of a cathedral.

Eddie whispered, "The Singing Place." Then he yelled, *"The Singing Place. We found it!"*

In the distance, he saw a lighted spire...and began running toward it.

Jorge Mendoza sat huddled, staring out the station wagon window.

As Julie glanced at Dr. Finnegan there was a strange fear in her eyes. "How does he know my brother the way he does? I mean, every word, every look."

"I can't answer that. All I can tell you is that he may have seen him today."

Jorge barely heard them. Enraptured, he watched surreal rainbow lights that flashed and flowed from the traffic. In his head echoed the eerie music of the city.

"Lights. Lights. Music. Everywhere. So-so-so beautiful...No words, no words. So scared."

Julie looked at him, "What is he saying?"

"I think maybe he's saying that your brother lives in a world that only he can see filled with light and color, but he has no words to tell you about it. And he was very frightened."

"When I took him out yesterday morning, he didn't seem frightened. He just seemed stubborn like usual. But maybe that's the way I wanted to see him. Maybe I've never really seen him at all."

Suddenly, Jorge's attention jerked up to the sunroof, and a huge smile came to his face. He jabbed his finger upward.

"Hey. Hey-hey-hey-hey. Mr. Bunley. Mr. Bunley."

The little man was outside on the roof in a halo of mist, pounding to get in.

Julie just shook her head, "That's exactly what my brother said before he ran away. He has this imaginary friend, Mr. Bunley, from a book he loves."

Finnegan replied, "Do what you did this morning."

Jorge shrieked with laughter, "Up-up-up-up there. Can-I? Can-I?"

She opened the window, "This is so weird."

Instantly, Mr. Bunley slid into the car but only Jorge could see him. He began singing over and over, "Eddie, Eddie, it's time to get ready, we'll find a place to play. Eddie, Eddie, it's time to get ready, we've got to run away."

Mr. Bunley jumped into the back seat, motioning for him to follow.

"In-the-back. Can-I? Can-I?"

Tears were in Julie's eyes, "It's like he was riding with us yesterday morning."

Finnegan was watching Jorge very closely. "He's seeing things that we can't see. Tell him exactly what you told Eddie."

"Okay, you can get in the back, but don't start crawling around."

Jorge lumbered over the seat. Now everything turned to chaos as Mr. Bunley and Jorge crawled back and forth.

"Keep talking to him, Julie."

"Eddie, please. I'm going to have a wreck. Stop it."

"Mr. Bunley's tickling. Stop-it-stop-it-stop-it-stop-it-stop-it."

"Oh God..."

Jorge laughed, then, suddenly, he was quiet. He crouched on the floor. Squatting next to him, the little man whispered urgently, "Eddie, Eddie...It's time to get ready. We've got to run away."

"I-know-I-know-I-know-I-know-I-know-
I-know-I-know-I-know. Now? Right now?
Right-right-right-now?"

Mr. Bunley nodded very seriously.

"Scared. Scared-scared."

The weird little man smiled, "There'll be a
smile on every face. I'll pull a rabbit from a vase.
But we have to find The Singing Place. The Singing Place. The Singing Place."

Jorge whispered, "Okay-okay-I'll do it. I'll-
do-it- I'll-do-it. Find The Singing-Place."

Julie strained to hear, "What did he say?"

Finnegan leaned toward her. "He said, find
The Singing Place. Do you know what that
means?"

Julie stared at the doctor. "It's the name of
his favorite book." Suddenly, a light dawned.
"That's what Eddie called my mother's church.
She sang in the choir."

"When was the last time he was there?"

"A week ago for her funeral."

"Is it far away?"

"Only a few miles."

She exited the freeway.

Gasping for air, Eddie Gartman ran up the steps of the cathedral. Somewhere inside, a choir was singing.

"We found it. We found it. Mr. Bunley, where are you?"

From the tower high above, the carillon began to play again. Eddie looked up enraptured.

"It's so beautiful."

Walking up the steps, he entered the church and stood listening. Tears began running down his cheeks.

"Mommy...where...where...?"

Suddenly, he heard Mr. Bunley's voice, but it was distant and echoing.

"We'll put a smile on every face. But we've got to find the Singing Place...the Singing Place...the Singing Place..."

Eddie walked over to the stairs leading up to the bell tower.

"Mr. Bunley, where are you? Are you up there?"

He began climbing.

As Julie Gartman's station wagon pulled to a stop in front of the cathedral, the carillon was still playing.

Jorge stared at the church. In his mind he heard even more beautiful music, almost as though angels were singing.

Julie shook her head, "Why didn't I think of this. Of course, he'd want to come here. He loved the choir and the bells."

In Eddie's reality, Jorge saw wonderful colored lights everywhere. Then his eyes grew wide. Mr. Bunley was standing on the steps of the church, motioning for him to come.

Jorge was thrilled, "This-this-is-it. Okay-okay-okay-okay. Here, here, now."

Jumping out of the car, he ran up the stairs and disappeared into the building. Julie and Dr. Finnegan got out and followed.

Inside the cathedral, through Eddie's eyes, Jorge saw the room filled with a mist of silvery light and shadows. It was as though the music of Heaven was flowing everywhere.

He whispered, "Mommy, mommy."

As he stared toward the front, in the mist there appeared a casket surrounded with candles. "Mommy..."

Jorge started toward it, but, suddenly, Mr. Bunley called to him.

"Eddie, Eddie, come on and get ready, there's nowhere left to stay. Eddie, Eddie, come on and get ready, it's time to fly away."

Jorge turned. Mr. Bunley was on the spiral staircase leading up into the bell tower. Grinning and motioning, he began to climb. Jorge followed.

Outside, Julie Gartman was about to enter the cathedral, when Dr. Finnegan stopped her.

"Wait. Ms. Gartman, before you go in, there's something you should know. I...don't know what you'll find in there."

"What do you mean?"

He struggled for words. "I'm a surgeon. In my practice, I've seen cases that were hopeless, where there was nothing anyone could do. Yet...something happened. I never wanted to call them miracles. I was afraid of the word, but that's what they were. There have been times in the operating room, where I could almost feel... someone...present, as though an invisible hand were guiding mine."

"I don't understand what you're saying. What does this have to do with my brother?"

"I'm saying there may be a world outside the one we see and sometimes it reaches through and touches ours. When you walk into that church--if your brother is there--there's a chance that you'll see him as you never have before."

"What do you mean?"

"Maybe nothing. Maybe we've made a mistake and we've wasted your time. I don't know.

You said your mother came here often. Did she...pray for Eddie?"

"Every day of her life."

"Then...as you go in...remember those prayers."

With a strange look, Julie Gartman entered the church. Much more slowly, Dr. Finnegan followed.

The carillon had stopped playing but the unseen choir still sang. Jorge reached the top of the spiral staircase and stepped into the moonlit tower. Silver mist was everywhere. For a moment, he stood, enraptured, listening to the music in his mind and singing with it.

"La-la-la-la-la-la. Music-music-music. La-la-la la-la."

Then he turned. Someone was looking at him. A few feet away, Eddie Gartman stood in the shadows. Their eyes met. The transformation was complete.

Eddie whispered, "It was you. You were the one in the room with the mirrors."

But there was no recognition in Jorge's eyes. He started singing loudly, "La-la-la-la-la-la-la..."

Suddenly, Eddie heard a woman's voice calling to him from down below inside the church.

"Eddie? Eddie, are you up there?"

He looked down and saw Julie.

"Yes."

Julie saw her brother above in the tower, but his face was in the shadows.

"Eddie? Oh, thank God." She started to cry. "I have been looking for you everywhere. Please, come down right now."

Slowly, Eddie Gartman began descending. As he made his way down the stairs, his face remained hidden. But the closer he got, the more Julie could see that he had changed. His body was slimmer and taller and there was no limp.

"Eddie? Is that you? What's happened?"

A few steps from the bottom, his face entered the light.

"Julie."

Julie saw, but she couldn't believe what she saw. Almost unable to breathe, she whispered, "My God, my God, my God..."

Softly, Eddie spoke to her, "I was in a room of mirrors and stars. A man came in. Something happened. He touched my head and I began to wake up."

He stared around. "The lights and music. Nothing is soft anymore."

Julie couldn't move. All she could do was stare at him. Slowly, Eddie walked into the sanctuary and looked toward the front. Tears filled his eyes.

"Mommy was in this place...down at the front...with candles all around. But she's gone now, isn't she?"

Julie was crying silently. "Yes."

"I remember...but it's like a dream. Will she ever come back?"

Julie shook her head.

Slowly, his tears fell, the lost tears, the tears that could never come, because to mourn is to understand.

"Before she left...did she know...that I loved her?"

Julie whispered, "Oh yes, she knew."

Taking him in her arms, they cried together.

Jorge Mendoza stood in the bell tower singing. He looked down. On the floor at his feet were Eddie's book and blanket. He picked them up. Then, he heard Mr. Bunley's echoing voice.

"Eddie, Eddie, come on and get ready. It's time to have some fun. Eddie, Eddie, come on and get ready, we'll run and run and run."

Jorge looked out. Mr. Bunley was on the roof, motioning for him to follow.

"There'll be a smile on every face. I'll pull a rabbit from a vase. But we have to fly to The

Singing Place, The Singing Place, The Singing Place."

Jorge started to climb out onto the roof. Down below, Dr. Finnegan saw and yelled, *"Jorge, no! Don't go out there!"*

But Jorge didn't hear him. All he heard was the singing voice in his mind. Dr. Finnegan rushed up the stairs.

As though in a dream, Jorge followed Mr. Bunley across the roof. The stars over the city seemed to swirl as though the depths of the universe were descending to earth.

The doctor reached the top of the bell tower and climbed out. *"Jorge, come back!"*

Standing at the edge of the roof, Jorge looked up at the sky. Another step and he would fall to his death. In front of him, Mr. Bunley's face hovered in the darkness.

"Eddie, Eddie, come on and get ready, it's time...to jump...and fly."

As he struggled across the roof, Finnegan yelled, *"Jorge...turn around and look at me!"*

But he didn't. With a smile, he was about to step into the air.

But, suddenly, there was a whisper of thunder and a distant lightning flash. Jorge's eyes grew wide. Mr. Bunley disappeared. Out of the universe fell shafts of brilliance that moved toward him. In them was a great Pillar of Golden Light.

Closer and closer it came, until it was directly above. Then, slowly, it descended. In the mist was One whose body seemed made of Light. From Him streamed overwhelming glory. Drawing close, He reached out His hand.

In His palm there was a hole that flowed with blood. He lifted it. Gently, onto Jorge's face fell drops of crimson drenched with the Love of God.

Tears came into Jorge's eyes and a transformation began. One by one, the softly misshapen features vanished and his eyes became clear.

Dr. Finnegan was making his way very cautiously across the roof. All he saw was Jorge looking up into the darkness.

"Jorge..."

Slowly, Jorge turned...and their eyes met. All the marks of what had happened were gone. His face was what it had been, except for one thing. The terrible scar remained. Jorge looked down toward the ground. On the steps of the church, looking up at him were Eddie and Julie Gartman.

CHAPTER FIFTEEN

Gifts

The sun was setting. Once more, Jorge Mendoza stood alone on the broken pier. As he listened to the roar of the surf, he was deep in thought.

Dr. Finnegan's Mercedes pulled into the parking lot. Jorge turned and watched as the doctor got out. He was carrying a package. Finnegan joined him.

"You wrecked a good pier."

"Yes and I'm glad the city doesn't know who did it."

"How are you feeling?"

"I'm fine." But there was sadness in his eyes.

"So what are you thinking about?"

"I just want to remember this place when I am gone."

Finnegan handed him the package. "This came to the hospital for you."

Jorge opened it. Inside was the 'Mr. Bunley' book.

"He was an ugly little man. I think it's time for Mr. Bunley to go for a swim with my puppets." He sailed the book out into the ocean. "Did you talk to them?

"Yes, they're leaving for Chicago the day after Christmas."

"And what are they telling people?"

"The police think he was found by his sister. The neighbors believe he's going to a residential home out of state. No one who knew him before will see him. He'll have a new life."

Jorge nodded and stared out at the water. "I hope he'll be happy. The world he lost was beautiful, but so lonely and this one is so hard. After his mother died, Mr. Bunley was his only friend."

"Well, I'm sure he's going to have a lot more friends now. He has a few years of catching up to do. He doesn't even know how to read." He paused, "Will it ever come back to you, Jorge?"

Jorge shook his head. "I don't think so."

"How do you know?"

"I could feel when it left. I don't think it's ever in one person for very long. It's too much for anyone except Jesus. When it comes again, it will be to someone else. I didn't want it. I fought it. But I am so glad that God is wiser and more powerful than me."

The doctor was silent for a moment, "I'm not a religious person, what do I know? But maybe it only comes at Christmas."

"I don't think it's because of Christmas. I think many strange things are going to happen before Jesus comes again."

"Those flying things you saw, you call them angel vultures. I haven't been able to sleep very well since you told me about them."

"They are real, Dr. Finnegan."

"Where do they come from?"

"A place of terrible darkness. They do not cause all of our suffering. They didn't make Ginny and Eddie the way they were, but when we are in pain it gives them pleasure. But Jesus is stronger than they are. I wish you believed in him, doctor."

"Well, maybe someday I will. But speaking of Jesus. Christmas is the day after tomorrow. I wonder if you'd reconsider doing that puppet show?"

Jorge shook his head sadly, "My plane leaves tomorrow night. Even if I was here, I couldn't do it alone."

"I thought you'd say that, so I brought you some help."

Finnegan pointed toward the parking lot. Standing beside the doctor's car, was a dark, attractive woman holding a little girl. But the little girl refused to be held any longer. Jumping down, she ran toward her father.

As though in a dream, Jorge stared. Then the tears came. "Oh, God...thank you."

He swept his daughter into his arms and then ran to his wife.

Dr. Finnegan turned back toward the ocean and smiled.

As Ana Mendoza looked up at her husband, she was crying. Her finger gently traced his scar. "Oh, my love, what has happened to you?"

Jorge smiled, "Now I am very, very ugly."

She shook her head, "No. I don't know why, but that is the most beautiful thing I have ever seen."

Christmas day.

A hospital ward filled with children was decorated with snowflakes, teddy bears and stockings. In a corner, stood a large tree. Under it were dozens of presents. The children, with their doctors and nurses, were watching a wonderful puppet show.

A little girl named Maria sat with a little girl named Ginny, while the puppets told a wonderful story about the beginning of the greatest miracle, the first Christmas of long ago.

Across the city, a cathedral was decorated for Christmas. Many people were gathered listening to a choir. In a pew toward the front, sat Julie and Eddie Gartman. As he listened to the music, Eddie looked up at the great crucifix that hung above them. Julie watched him, then looked where he was looking…at the face of Jesus. Her eyes filled with tears.

As Eddie listened, suddenly, the singing deepened until it was like a choir of angels. A strange look came into his eyes.

He stared down at his hand. Across it rippled a faint glow. He turned it over. In his palm appeared a hole filled with brilliant light. Slowly, the color deepened into crimson, and the light became a drop of blood.

In Memory of Virginia May Luck

24 March 1951 – 10 January 2006

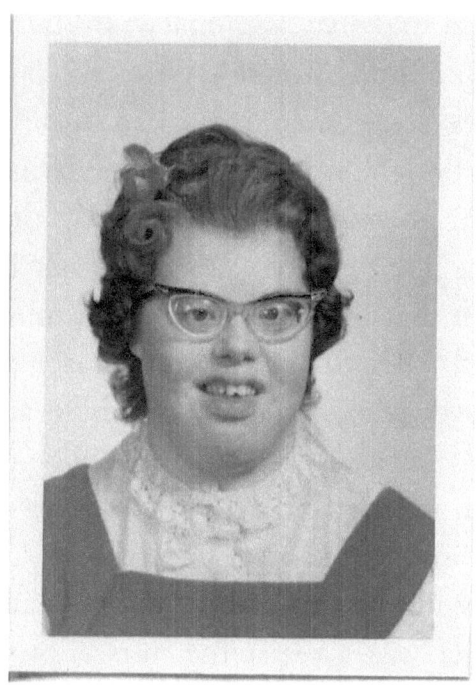

(Written the week after my sister died.)

I remember the day we brought her home from the hospital. Though I was only five, I vividly recall standing in the back seat of our car with my younger brother Bill, looking over with great curiosity at the baby in my mother's arms. I remember my father telling us that this was our new little sister Virginia May. My parents had wanted a daughter for so long. My mother was 40 when Virginia was born. Back then no one knew the risks of such a pregnancy.

As we rode home from the hospital, my brother and I were told that Virginia was different from other babies. Our family would have to take care of her for the rest of her life. Of course, I had no idea what he was talking about. She looked like a regular baby to me. But Virginia had been born with Down Syndrome.

The fact that we were taking her home at all was unusual in that day. Out of their infinite storehouse of wisdom, the doctors had told my parents that my sister would never walk or talk. She would remain a human vegetable and the wisest thing would be to put her in an institution where she could live out her short miserable existence under the care of strangers. To their eternal credit, my mother and father rejected such ugly lunacy. My mother was a registered nurse. She knew how to take care of babies. And my father, well, he had always wanted a daughter. Since Virginia was the one God had given he was going to take joy in her no matter what.

That day as we drove home from the hospital, I didn't realize it, but our family had been changed forever. Together we began to climb jagged hills of joy and sorrow. For the most part, the joy came from my father who made his little girl the center of his life at home.

Very quickly, we discovered that my parents had been right. Virginia was anything but a vegetable. She might have "special needs" as we say today, but that didn't preclude her from having a strong personality. Over those first years Virginia learned to talk, sing songs, and in general communicate her desires quite effectively. This was due to my mother's wonderful physical care combined with much loving time spent by my father who taught her all he could. But he was a busy professor at the Moody Bible Institute of Chicago. Teaching the Bible brought little money and often he had to work late, so his time at home was limited.

My sister's birth was the beginning of real suffering for my mother. And much of that suffering she did alone. Her response to Virginia's condition was unmitigated sorrow. Back in 1950, it wasn't known that Down Syndrome was caused by a genetic defect. So, for many years, my mother believed that Virginia had been injured at birth by a careless doctor. Even when the evidence to the contrary was overwhelming, it took decades for her to begin to accept it.

With grim determination, she committed her life to protecting and caring for the child God had given. But her broken heart did not mend.

When Down Syndrome children are small, they are cute and loveable. And that's the way my sister was through her early years. For a while, her health was fragile. Several times during infancy, it took all of my mother's nursing skill to keep her alive. But, finally, she became quite healthy.

In the 1950's families with "retarded" children didn't take them out very often. Soon I understood why. As I grew older, I began to realize that when we were at church or in a restaurant people stared at Virginia. I came to hate those stares. They made me angry. But I understood why they were staring. My sister looked strange. Though I loved her deeply, slowly I began to dread being seen with her in public. It didn't help that, like many children with her condition, she developed a whole series of odd quirks, such as wrapping a napkin and string around a stick and swinging it endlessly in front of her while she made grunting noises.

As a teenager I found it quite horrible when it happened outside of our home. When you're a teenage boy filled with insecurity, sitting in a restaurant next to someone who is swinging a stick and grunting is not where you want to be. How can you get a cute girl to look at you when she's transfixed by the manifold oddities of your sister? There were times when I felt like our whole family must look retarded.

As I remember the years of childhood, I think it was very difficult for my brother and me. In countless ways, our home was a good one. My mother and father loved us deeply. They cared for our physical needs and instilled values that have guided me over my entire life. But our little sister took so much time that there wasn't a lot left for two rowdy boys. Our father left for work before the family awoke and worked late several evenings each week. Our mother didn't drive and didn't feel that she could leave Virginia with anyone, so she stayed at home, which meant that we were on our own.

For most of the little events of our lives, whether sports for my brother Bill, or various kinds of dramatic performances for me, our parents just weren't there. Now don't get me wrong, I wasn't always unhappy about being on my own. It meant that I was free to do pretty much as I pleased. As the years passed "doing what I pleased" gave me the reputation of being the "bad" kid of the family.

As an adult, it's normal to look back and try to understand your childhood. As I look back the hardest thing to deal with for me was my mother's anger and sorrow. Many times I remember waking up in the middle of the night to hear her sobbing as she worked alone in the kitchen.

Children don't understand such experiences. They tend to blame themselves for whatever is wrong. As a young child, seeing my mother in such agony made me afraid. When a child is afraid and there's nothing he can do to change the situation, often he responds with anger of his own. I think I was angry through much of my childhood and didn't really know it.

This led to a kind of rebellion. Mainly it was expressed with extreme laziness, which included doing very badly in school. But one form of rebellion turned into an unexpected gift. I had a vivid imagination. So when I faced unpleasant circumstances and emotions, it was easy to vanish into a world of my own. I would tell myself endless fascinating stories. Ultimately, from that form of escape, came my career as a writer.

My parents nicknamed my sister Gingy. I never liked the name. I thought it was ugly. But Gingy is what we called her. As she began to grow up, with my father's joyful presence, Gingy developed a delightfully loving personality.

For the first 25 years of her life she sang and laughed as her world slowly expanded. Wonderful teachers tried to help her learn. In her late teens, she began attending a workshop where she found many friends. (Have you ever been to a Halloween costume party with 20 Down Syndrome adults? It is truly unforgettable.)

People at church and in the neighborhood loved Gingy. She was a cheerful happy little soul. Then, in March of 1976, a great tragedy struck our family. My father passed away. He had been in the hospital in traction with a broken leg. During the weeks that he was confined to bed, a blood clot had formed. When they got him up to put on a cast it went to his lungs and heart and he was gone.

By that time I was married. My wife, Carel and I had three children and were living in a town near my parents. I will never forget the day of my father's passing. I drove over to the workshop to pick up my sister.

On the way home, I tried to tell her what had happened, that our dad had gone to be with Jesus in Heaven and we wouldn't see him again in this world. Of course, she didn't understand a word that I was saying. I remember feeling a profound loneliness. At that moment more than anything I wanted a sister I could talk to.

People with Virginia's condition don't mourn like the rest of us. It took her a long time to understand that our dad was really gone. About the time my mother was beginning the first steps of healing, Gingy was entering her time of sorrow. And her mourning went on for years. My father had been the light of her life. For a very long time, she cried every day for him.

After his death, Virginia's personality slowly began to change. She was still very loving, but the bubbling happiness passed away. Like every member of our family, she had tended toward stubbornness. Now it became a major trait of her life. Often this created some horrifying and hilarious situations.

If Gingy decided that she liked a particular location, well, that's where she would stay. If she liked church she would sit in the pew for hours after the service had ended and no amount of coaxing or coercion could get her to move an inch.

Like many Down Syndrome people, a lethargic lifestyle led to significant weight gain. If she didn't want to move, it was almost impossible to move her. This led to a number of interesting experiences, such as Gingy sitting in a restaurant for hours or Gingy sitting in a stall in a women's room as though it had become her new home.

There was the time Gingy flew to California with my mother. They needed to change planes in L.A. to continue on to Fresno and our mountain home. But when she entered the terminal in L.A. she decided that this was the end of the journey. She sat down and no one, from my mother to several large security personnel, could get her to move. Such experiences were lessons in patience and, in retrospect, most were hilarious. I say *in retrospect*. But when you're driving hundreds of miles to pick up your mother and sister because your sister forced them to miss a flight, the humor can escape you.

Our family is full of "Gingy stories." Like the time we all went to Chicago to experience the Chinese New Year. The parade was in Chinatown. We were walking back to our car. Gingy was with my brother. On the street, we passed a little group of venerable Chinese ladies conversing in their native language. Filled with wonder, my sister stopped and stared. Never had she heard anything like it.

Thinking this must be some kind of game – old ladies babbling at each other – she decided to join in. Rushing over she stuck her face between them and started babbling too. Then, she laughed uproariously. Neither my brother nor I quite had the courage to go and extract her from her new fascination. My wife, Carel, had to do it.

Then, there was the time that Gingy vanished. She and my mother had been visiting in California for several months. My mother had taken a small apartment on a second floor. She had decided to move to the first floor, so we were helping her make the transition. Finally ready to bring Gingy down to her new residence, my oldest son and his friend went up to get her. A few minutes later, they came back in shock.

Gingy was gone. She had vanished from the apartment.

It seemed impossible. The last thing my sister would do would be to go out and wander off. She hated getting out of her chair. Unable to believe she was gone,

I rushed up to the apartment to see for myself before we called the police. Sure enough, the room was empty except for a couch, a chair, and an end table. On the floor under the table were two large pillows.

Wait a minute. There was something wrong with this picture. My mother didn't own any pillows.

Upon closer examination, I discovered that they weren't pillows at all. It was my sister's rather expansive posterior. She had always had the most amazing ability to fold herself in half. And that's what she had done. She had fallen asleep on the floor under the table, folded completely in half, face-down between her legs with only her bottom sticking out. And it looked exactly like two pillows.

There are so many stories about Gingy. It's so hard to believe that this wonderful, loving, quirky person is gone from us. From the moment she entered our lives we were changed forever. She taught us patience, love and compassion. She also taught us to have a strong taste for dark humor. I think almost every family with someone like Virginia will know what I mean. At certain moments, you've just got to laugh hysterically at the embarrassment and frustration.

C. S. Lewis once called certain kinds of suffering a "severe mercy." In all of her suffering and in the suffering that we experienced together, Virginia was a gift to us. And I'm very thankful for that gift. Her life has enriched mine in so many ways. Certainly, it has enriched my writing. A script that I have written that means so much to me is called "The Singing Place." It's about a young man with Down Syndrome who finds miraculous healing.

For every family with a Down Syndrome child, that is the Impossible Dream. Your loved one healed! If only it could happen, what would he or she be like...at this age...and this age...and this one?

Virginia gave us all the love that she had to give. And there was a lot in her. There's something else that you should know. My little sister loved Jesus. From her earliest years my father and mother taught her about Him. She sang His songs and learned about His love in simple Bible stories.

Though she could never read, for years Gingy carried around a little New Testament. Every page was folded and messed up, because she would sit for hours and leaf carefully through it, somehow knowing how important it was, though not understanding why. Her New Testament is now a cherished family possession.

As a Christian, my hope goes far beyond this world. Jesus died for my sins and the sins of my sister. And He promised Eternal Life to all who would believe in Him. With utterly child-like faith, Gingy believed. One of the great glories of Christianity is that it's for all people, even ones like my sister. If going to Heaven required her to do anything, she would never get there. If earning her own salvation was the only way for God to accept her, she would have no hope.

But of all the religions of the world Christianity is the only one with a Loving God who came to this earth as the Good Shepherd and who reaches down with gentle compassion to the littlest and most damaged of His lambs.

To the Christian, this life is only the beginning. While I sorrow for my sister, in my heart there is a deep joy. What a moment! When Jesus came into her hospital room and called the real Virginia out of that broken dying body that had been her burden for so long.

What an awakening! To be able to think and speak clearly, to remember and see and know! What a meeting when she entered the Gates of Heaven. I know that waiting there for her was our dad. Finally, his daughter in all of her beauty, has come home.

I used to imagine that if Gingy had been born with a normal mind and body she would have been a brilliant and beautiful woman. Maybe she would have had a blazing career, a loving husband and children. (Often she would ask my mother when she was going to get married.) In this world such blessings were not for her. But in the next, her blessings will be far greater and they will never end.

This much I know. My sister is not lost. Someday I'm going to walk with her through golden streets in the Great City of Jesus our King. In that wonderful place, we'll walk and talk for a long, long time. And there will be so much to talk about because, after all, we will have a lifetime of catching up to do.

Blessings on you sweet little sister. Goodbye...for now.

About the Author

Coleman Luck is a Hollywood writer and executive producer known for such TV series as "The Equalizer" and "Gabriel's Fire." He is a mentalist and a member of the Academy of Magical Arts at The Magic Castle in Hollywood. His first novel, <u>Angel Fall</u>, was published in 2009 by Zondervan, a subsidiary of Harper/Collins. His second novel, <u>The Mentalist Prophecies - Book One – Dagon's Illusion,</u> was published in 2013. He is the author of <u>Proof of Heaven? A Mental Illusionist Examines the Afterlife Experience of Eben Alexander M.D. from a Biblical Viewpoint</u> and <u>The Curse of Conservatism.</u>

Coleman studied the Bible at the Moody Bible Institute, received his undergraduate degree from Northern Illinois University (magna cum laude) and did graduate study at NIU, the University of Southern California and Simon Greenleaf School of Law. Coleman and his wife of 47 years, Carel Gage Luck, a fine artist, live in the mountains of central California.

Visit his website: www.colemanluck.com.

www.ingramcontent.com/pod-product-compliance
Lightning Source LLC
Chambersburg PA
CBHW020128180626
46810CB00004B/1450